New Tales
by
Uncle Harry

Keith Garvey

Cover design by Allan Cornwell and Rosie van der Elst

Titles in the series:

Tall Tales from the Bush Volume 1 ISBN 1 875 169 31 8
Tall Tales from the Bush Volume 2 ISBN 1 875 169 32 6
Tall Tales from the Bush Volume 3 ISBN 1 875 169 33 4
ISBN 1 875 169 34 2 (Set)

Printed in Australia by McPherson's Printing Group

Produced for the National Direct Marketing Group by:
Allan Cornwell
25 Churchill Road
Mt. Martha Vic 3934

National Direct Marketing Group:
Books Plus (VIC/SA)
Books First (NSW/QLD)
Premier Books (WA)
Meander Books (TAS)

To the Glen Innes Bandits,
who I greatly admire and respect

Jo
Gingerbread
Taffy
Firth
Kelley
Ned
Katie

Also by Keith Garvey

The Funny Bugger.
Shout for the Adder.
Slowly Sweats the Gun.
Where the Blacksoil Ends.
Night of the Dingo.
My Uncle Harry.
Uncle Harry Rides Again.
Uncle Harry Returns.
More Tales of Uncle Harry.

Rhymes of a Ratbag.
Ditties of a Deadbeat.
Blacksoil Ballads.
Absolutely Australian Verses.
Songs of a Shearer.
Digger Ditties.
Cattle-Camp Collection.

Dinkum Little Aussies.
Vanishing Australians.
Verses of a Vagrant.
The Keith Garvey Omnibus.
The Bunyip Wakes.

Contents

Contents

The Superstrong Snake

"Landholders are pretty careful with their money", I remarked to Uncle Harry. "A carpet snake couldn't squeeze a high wage out of them".

"Don't be too sure", the old boy replied. "Carpet snakes have amazin' powers of constriction. If a big one throws a few coils round yer ribs he can squash yer ribs to powder in a matter of seconds".

"I suppose you've seen this happen", I said innocently.

"Not exactly", Harry replied. "But I once witnessed a terrific feat of strength by a big carpet. I still shiver with fear when I think about it.

"I was rabbitin' at the time, on a property near Graman. There was a shearin' shed near me camp, and close by a lot of farmin' gear was stacked, includin' a forty-four gallon steel drum, full of petrol.

"I had a pretty cunnin' dog at the time called Nosey, on account of his keen sense of smell. He would sniff at the openin' of a burrow, and yer could bet if he wagged his tail there was a rabbit inside it. If he walked away lookin' disgusted there was no way it was inhabited.

"One day I was skinnin' a few bunnies when I hears a string of yelps, and Nosey flies out of the bush runnin' for dear life. Right behind him is gallopin' a big carpet snake about fifteen feet long.

"Nosey heads for the petrol drum, dodges behind it then keeps on goin'. The snake must have thought the dog was hidin' in the drum, because he throws a couple of coils round the drum and starts squeezin'.

"Holy Smoke, boy, let me tell yer the pressure that serpent applied was unbelievable. the bung flew out of the drum and petrol ran everywhere. Yer could hear the scream of the tortured steel as the drum collapsed. I stood sort of paralysed with fear, then a startlin' thing happened. The friction was so great that sparks were struck off the metal, and the petrol caught fire. There was a sheet of flame and a big bang. When the fire died down there was nothin' left of that old snake but a few ashes. An unbelievable happenin''.

"Unbelievable is right", I said.

"I'm glad you agree", Harry replied. "only for seein' it I wouldn' have believed it possible".

CIVILIZATION
1000 MILES

Dangerous Reptiles

"Funny thing how a lot of people are scared of snakes", Uncle Harry remarked. "And the wild legends that grow up about them are also funny".

"What brought snakes to your mind?", I queried.

Harry points to a deep patch of shade, where a small pied ring-snake (called bandy-bandy by bushmen) lay between the roots of a curricabah. The old boy filled his pipe with great deliberation.

"Now take the bandy-bandy, for instance. A reptile practically non-venomous. But people tell yer that if he bites yer, yer take a fit for every ring on his body. Rubbish!".

Harry puffed smoke and gazed at the tiny snake, it's body circled with black and white rings. At last he looked up.

"Just the same", he said, "I remember a case where a bandy-bandy killed a bloke without even bitin' him".

"Impossible", I said.

"The tale is a bit complicated, but never the less true", Harry said. "There was this bloke we called Active, on account of he was the laziest coot under the sun. Had a downtrodden wife and four or five kids, and they were always half-starvin' because Active wouldn't work. All he wanted to do was drink grog and sleep.

"Now Active had a deadly fear of snakes, so the wife deciced to put a scare in him, hopin' he'll change his ways. So she waits 'til he goes off to the pub, takin' what few bob the family possessed. Then she searches round the bush 'til she finds a bandy-bandy. She kills it and takes it home. There was lots of cat-head weed growin' round the place, so she grabs two big cat heads as well.

"Active comes home stonkered and falls inter bed, and the wife puts the cat-heads and the dead snake in his boot. Next mornin' Active rises hoarse and thirsty, and sticks his foot in the boot. The cat-heads stuck in his big toe, and with a yell he pulls the boot off and spots the bandy-bandy.

"I'm bit! I'm bit!!" he yells, and collapes on the floor. The neighbours all rush over, spot the snake and the toe with two bleedin punctures in it, and they panic and sends for the doctor, the police, the ambulance and God knows what else. One old sinner starts tellin' Active that he'll go inter convulsions then his brain will bust from the venom. By the time the doctor gets there, Actice is as dead as Pontias Pilate. Just goes to show yer how quick fright can kill a man.

"The doctor does a quick examination, and finds death was caused by snakebite. The widow soon found another bloke, this one with a bit of money and property, so she was in clover. Used to spend all her spare time supportin' a society for the preservation of reptiles. And around that town ever after, the harmless little bandy-bandy was regarded as bein' deadlier than the Indian Cobra".

"And how do regard snakes, old uncle?", I asked.

Harry grinned around his pipe. "Yer don't have to worry about the ones in the bush. Yer gotter watch the two-legged ones. Especially the female of the species".

The Everlasting Flame

"Old timers tell me", I remarked to Uncle Harry, "That the roots of a mallee tree can burn for more than a week if covered up with ashes".

"Mallee wood is certainly long-burning", the old boy replied. But it doesn't burn as long as the myall wood that yer find round here. Myall roots burn for a great time, and give off a fragrant smoke".

"Totally different from that foul pipe of yours", I said sourly.

"You don't realise how invigorating my pipe is". Harry grinned. "A couple of draws on it when you feel off colour, and it makes you a new man".

"I'd rather think it would make me a dead man", I replied.

"Let's leave my pipe alone and get back to long-burning wood", Harry said. "Once me and Stevo were sinkin' an earth tank near North Star. We were camped in an old tin hut with an open galley. There was plenty of wood around, and we always had a good fire goin'. The morning we finished the job, Stevo threw a myall root on the fire, a big hard twisted one. We had a feed and got ready to leave.

"No need to put the fire out, mate", Stevo says. "She can't get away. Soon burn herself out".

"We headed the bullocks for home, and a lot of time went by. We worked at all kinds of job, and after five years the bloke we sunk the tank for sent word that he wanted it scooped out. We packs up and sets sail.

"On arrivin' we finds the old tin hut in a sad state of decay, but smoke was risin' out of the galley, and we reckoned some bloke was camped there".

"We gotter move him, mate", Stevo says. "Ain't room in there for three of us".

"We enters the door and that was when we got the shock of our lives! The old hut's interior was no different from when we left it. Dust and cobwebs everywhere. And

11

on the fire, still burnin', is the myall root that Steveo put there five long years ago".

"Come off it", I said. "Someone must have been around the place a day before, and lit the fire again".

"No boy", Harry said solemnly. "It was the same root Steveo put there. I could tell be the curious twists and knots on it. So yer see, myall wood will burn indefinitely".

"A pity your pipe won't do the same", I replied. "You wouldn't have a tobacco bill every month".

Harry ignored my spiteful thrust, and wearing a sly grin, lit up and puffed steadily.

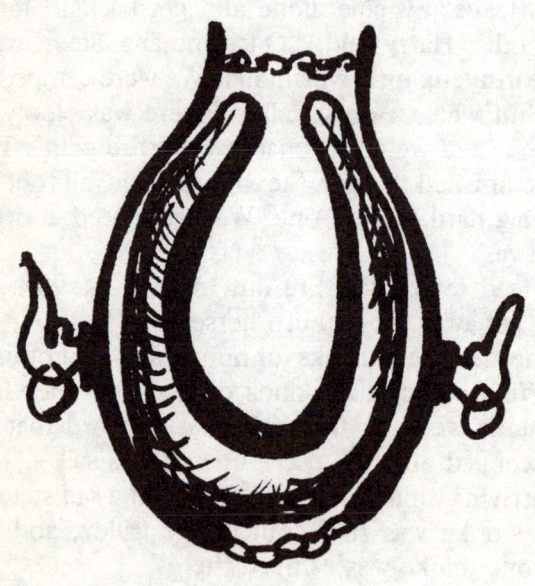

The Wampus Legend

The bunyip is well known throughout the bush, but Pallamallawa is the only place where I have heard of a wampus. The legend is very dead now, but when I was a schoolboy at the small village, many old hands believed that a weird creature lived in the Gwydir river, and it was referred to as the Wampus.

The first time I heard of it was in 1931, when an old and respected bushman claimed to have seen a large black creature like a walrus. At his appearance it grunted several times like a pig, then dived out of sight in the moonlit water. Our narrator was partial to rum, so it was decided that his monster was produced by alcohol.

Not long afterwards a fisherman of sober habits reported a strange creature with a horn on its nose, that sank to the depths on sighting him. There was also a respected but illiterate settler who saw the monster, and he claimed "itwuz different to a bunyip, more like a rinosorarse. It had a horn on its head, and a bunyip's got tusks. It was a wampus".

An exhaustive perusal of natural history books failed to turn up any creature called wampus, so where the appellation for the apparition came from I have no idea. For a long time in the village there were wampus believers and wampus detractors, while some who believed in the creature's existence refused to accept bunyips and vice versa. One knowledgeable cove, who had never been more than twenty miles from the village in his life, claimed it was a giant platypus, while others suggested freshwater whales, crocodiles, dungongs, dolphins, dinosaurs and even fish-men. But nothing was ever proved.

According to a popular belief, this mysterious beast was a vegetarian. All who claimed to have seen it agreed that it had no carniverous or violent habits like Bunyip. The wampus was, according to its supporters, a gentle and herbiverous creature, and ate only river weeds and vegetation.

There are still a few believers around the place, but nobody has seen the wampus for years, and people of the modern generation are unaware of the legend. But for what my opinion is worth, I feel that the wampus was a child of the old hands' imagination. But if Idi Amin was to come to our village and rise dripping from the Gwydir, there are still many gullible locals who would believe that this large and unlovable black beast was the legendary wampus.

14

The Sacred Goats

In an outback village where I once spent several months, lived the O'Phelan brothers, Mick, Jack and Paddy, three bushworkers of Irish descent. They were willing and capable toilers at any outback occupation, and deadly marksmen. Only one, Paddy was married. His wife Maggie was a readhead straight from the bogs of County Donegal, and she acted as cook and housekeeper for the family. A kind Christian soul, her ideas regarding religion were somewhat distorted. Because they are mentioned so much in the scriptures, she believed that goats had a deep religious significance, and to kill one was an unforgiveable sacrilege.

Times were hard, and cheap meat was hard to acquire. Paddy and brother Jack went off to a burning-off job some miles from the village, and Maggie warned them not to return without meat of some sort. On arriving at the job they found wild goats in abundance, and on finishing the contract Paddy shot a fat young nanny and dressed it out carefully.

"Remember it's a sheep", he warned Jack. "The old woman can't tell the difference, and what she don't know can't hurt her".

Maggie viewed the "sheep" with joy, but remarked that the flesh seemed darker than usual for such an animal. Paddy blandly informed her that this was due to grazing on a certain type of grass.

"Lamb" chops were the menu for Sunday dinner, Maggie remarking on the excellence of the "mutton". On Sunday afternoon, brother Mick arrive home from a shearing-shed, equipped with two bottles of wine. Both he and Jack were veterans of the first world war, and they began to imbibe, and re-live a few old Army memories. On being called to tea, both slightly intoxicated, they sat down to what Maggie unwittingly described as "leg of lamb". Before long Jack forgot himself, and wiping gravy from his long moustache, announced, ''by cripes this bloody goat's good, Mick''.

There was a stunned silence, then Maggie went into action. The leg of goat just missed Paddy's head as he made what he described afterwards as a strategic withdrawal. Jack and Mick went out the window with more speed than they had ever displayed going ''over the top in Flanders''. Pots, pan, pieces of goat and Gaelic curses followed their retreat.

Maggie's outraged sense of sacrilege caused her to go to evening Mass and ask absolution for her menfolk. Later she buried what was left of the goat, offering devout prayers. Late that night the boys silently returned, packed up and went bush for several days. Needless to say, any meat later acquired had to be delivered on the hoof.

Now as I conclude this quite authentic tale, I cannot help wondering if organised religion is as helpful as most of us think. I fail to see that it contains much value when absorbed by devout but semi-literate people.

Wayward Winds and Rafferty's Rules

"The football matches today", said Uncle Harry, "are like everything else in modern Australia. All the fun goes when the game gets too regimented. It's much more excitin' when Rafferty's rules apply. And yer see some amazin' happenins. I recall a game when the final issue was decided by a whirlwind".

"I don't doubt that there was a lot of wind blowing if you were there", I said.

Harry ignored my nasty insinuation and began to fill his pipe.

"The game I speak of", he began, "was between two little towns out in the central west. The home team was a man short, and though I always considered football a brutal, barbaric game, I agreed to fill the gap. The captain placed me on the left wing, as he was aware of me terrific pace.

"The two teams were evenly matched, and with only a few minutes left to full time, neither side had scored. Our full-back puts in a mighty punt that soars high in the air. I come from behind him like a bullet, racin' to get the ball, and also goin' after it is the opposin' winger. It was touch and go who was goin' to be first to the ball when it lands.

"Now I tell yer boy, that was a mighty kick the full-back put in, because when the ball landed, it busts. The leather case split down one side, and the rubber bladder flew out. In the scramble that follered I got hold of the bladder and headed for the goal-line. Straight as a rocket I goes, and plants the bladder between the posts. I looks round, thinkin' what a stroke I've done, and what d'yer think? The opposin' winger has scored at the other end with the football-case. Right under the bar.

"Nobody knew what was the correct procedure, so the ref decides to apply Rafferty's rules. He declares a three-all draw, but our captain questions him on the rulin'. "What about the goal kick", he says. "We have the right to try and convert".

"O.K." says the referee. "Since your man scored with the bladder, he can have a go at the goal with it. The oppositon can use the case".

"The opposition kicked first, but their man had no hope of puttin the case over the bar. Then our bloke places the bladder without much hope, and rushes in and kicks. Yer wouldn't believe what happened".

"One of them wild western whirlwinds comes along, got under the bladder and lefts it clean over the bar, and up went the linesmen's flags. Goal it was, our team wins by five to three, and off we go to the pub to celebrate".

"Are you sure you wasn't celebrating before the match?", I asked.

"Not at all", Harry replied. "We proved our superiority under Rafferty's rules. Of course, the whirl-wind was helpful".

The Mad Cook's Revenge

"Never underestimate the cunning of any bloke who appears to be a bit ratty", said Uncle Harry. "You'll mostly find they ain't as mad as they seem".

"What caused you to make this statement?", I asked.

"I was recalling a happening from along the track of my past life", Harry announced rather theatrically.

"A pretty dark, sinful track, I would imagine", I replied.

Harry lit his pipe, ignoring my nasty remark with lofty contempt.

"Somes fellers think it's funny to play a joke on a cove who's a bit lame under the hat", he began. But the job often misfires".

"I was at a shed near Surat once, pennin' up. The cook was a little bloke called Looney, and he wasn't sixteen ounces in the pound. One day the shearers killed a big tiger-snake near the shed. The joker that yer find in every team decided it would be a real joke to put the snake in Looney's bed while he was in the cook-house. The deed was silently done, and all the the gang were waitin' to see the result, but they were disappointed. There wasn't a sound from Looney's hut when he went to bed, and he never said a word at breakfast about snakes or anything else.

"Everyone was a bit baffled, wonderin' if the joke had misfired, and at tea that night Looney turns on a big pot of what he called "clear soup". I was never keen on fancy soups, so I passed it by in favour of corn junk and spuds, but the rest of the gang went at it hard and came back for seconds.

"We all heads for town on the cut out, and we're drinkin' in the railway bar when the train comes in. Looney boards the rattler, and we all wish him a good trip home. Just as the train pulls out, the joker yells, "who put the snake in the cook's bed?"

Looney leans out the carriage window. "I dunno who put the snake in the cook's bed", he sings out. "But I know who put the snake in the clear soup".

"Some of the gang starts to chase the train yellin' blue murder, but it had too much speed up and they had to come back. And they all had a sicky, bilious look about 'em. No doubt they were regrettin' the way they'd filled up on the snake soup.

"So always remember, boy", Uncle Harry concluded, "that it's hard to tell what's in a pot of soup, and it's harder to tell what's in the mind of any cove who's a bit ratty".

The Burial of Gutbuster

This grimly amusing little yarn was told to me by Jack, an old warrior who lived in a small bush community, and was a noted yarn teller and noted local historian. How greatly embellished the story is I would not know, but it is worth recording. I will present it in the style and manner that Jack told it.

*   *   *   *   *   *

I always remember that time old Gutbuster died. He was one of the toughest old coots I ever saw, in a land and time of tough people. I don't think he was conceived and born like anyone else. More likely the Lord hammered him out of angle-iron and strung him together with greenhide. So it was a big shock to all hands when he keeled over with a heart attack.

His family were pretty hard up, for it was despression days, but everyone did what they could to help. The biggest expense to be met was the hiring of the hearse. Gutbuster had died on the way to hospital in the nearest big town, which was twenty-five miles away, so it would be costly to get him back to the bush village. Tom, an old workmate, offered his services, or rather the service of his Chev Lorry, which was a top-class carriage in them times for both livin' and dead. Mick, another mate, decided to go along and help.

Both men were returned soldiers from the Kaiser's war. A pretty tough pair of heroes, they'd worked, drank and fought with Gutbuster on different occasions. I could never work out why they asked me to go along, as I was an overgrown boy of fourteen years, with the small amount of brains that bush kids of that age mostly possess.

We got to town O.K., but the men decided to have a nerve steadier at the Woolpack Hotel, the first pub west of town. Their nerves must have been bloody crook, because they had about six steadiers pretty quick. Then off to the undertakers to collect the coffin and go to the hospital for the body. The old lorry just didn't seem able to pass the Oasis Hotel, which was on the way.

"You can't park here with a coffin on the back", I said.

"Why not", Mick says. "Nobody's goin' to steal it. Yer get one all too soon".

When they surfaced half an hour later they both had a wet sail in the wind, and Tom had a bottle of Red Ned stickin' out of his hip-pocket.

We lobs at the hospital, and they shoulder the coffin. Instead of sneakin' quietly round the back to the morgue, they head straight for the front doors. Then Mick cast a shoe, stumbled and fell, and coffin and its bearers collapse on the lawn. They got up lookin' pretty staggery, got out the bottle, and sits on the coffin to take a reviver.

The doors flew open, and out rushes a fat little nurse. She was a pleasant lookin' girl, but too bloody overweight to be athletic. The way she floundered across the lawn made me think of a fat cross-bred sheep tryin' to get over a boggy creek. "Whatever are you men doing!", she puffed. "Take that casket around the back immediately. Who is it for?".

"It's to hold our mate Gutbuster, lady", Tom says. "The last suit he'll ever need".

"Kindly follow me", the girl says, and she leads off round the back ahead of the boys with the box, and yours truly bringin' up a bloody nervous rearguard action.

I'd never seen a dead body before, and the sight of the old warrior wrapped in a shroud shook me up some. But it didn't worry Tom and Mick. They dropped the box with a bang, Mick wobbled like a horse with stagger-heaves, and fell in the coffin. The little nurse really got upset.

"You men are disgracefully drunk", she says. "Why did you go drinking with a job like this to do?".

"Outa sorrer for our departed mate, lady", Mick says tearfully.

22

Tom was gazin' at the corpse with a tear in his eye like a travellin' rat. "You poor old bastard", he says. "Never again will you hit me with a jug of beer when we're havin' an argument. I forgive yer, old mate. Come on Mick. Lets get him in the box".

"You men are too drunk to do it," says the nurse. "This young lad and I will lift the body into the casket".

That realy put the wind up me. I had a crazy fear that Gutbuster would sit up and grab me if I touched him. But under the nurse's hard stare I took hold, and we did the job.

"Yer shoulda left it to Tom and me, lady", Mick says. "Over in Flanders we picked 'em up a leg at a time". He produced a bottle-opener and began to screw down the coffin-lid.

"If all our soldiers were like you two", came back the nurse, "It's a wonder the British won the battle. Now pull yourselves together and try to carry that casket out in a respectable manner. You should be ashamed".

Her tongue-bangin' must have had a soberin' effect, because they got the box on the lorry without further mishap. I reckoned on a safe trip home, but I overlooked one factor. We had to pass the Woolpack Hotel on the way. We didn't pass it.

Mick decided to park in and re-irrigate his pipes, and Tom agreed. By now it was pretty dark, and when the came out of the bar they discovered that the pin that went in the end of the crank-handle was missing. But this small mishap was soon overcome. Tom took a screw out of the coffin and used it as a pin for the crank. Several times on the way home they pulled up to have a drink, and the screw was always lost and another taken out of the coffin.

Once I tried to remonstrate, but Mick soon shut me up. "If yer don't shut up, I'll take Gutbusher out of the box and make yer nurse him all the way home".

That settled me. I was never happier to get home in me young life, and I swore I never would front as as undertaker's assistant again.

The old man had a big funeral next day, and two of

the pallbearers were Mick and Tom. Sober and quiet they were fair dinkum sorry to see the last of their old mate.

But I just wish their earlier method of mourning hadn't been so realistic.

Of Fogs and Dogs

"Fogs are a nuisance", said Uncle Harry, as he gazed at the thick grey mist that shrouded the tent.

"London fogs are the heaviest of all, so we are told", I replied.

The old boy gave a contemptuous glance, and stoked up his pipe.

"No fogs", he began, "are as heavy as those that come to the Monaro district. Thick as the dough for a damper, they are.

"I recall a time when me and Stevo were rabbitin' down there, near a place called Delegate. One mornin' we gets up and finds the camp so befogged that yer could cut slices out of the atmosphere and melt 'em in the camp-oven. We beat a path through the fog with a shovel to where the camp-fire was, gets her blazin' and swings the billy. Just then, away out in the fog, we hears a dingo howlin'. Stevo goes into the tent and gets his rifle. "What are yer goin' to do", I asks.

"Shoot that dog, mate", Stevo replies. "I can't see him, but I reckon if I aim at his howl I can down him".

"He squats down and waits, and soon the dingo howls again. Stevo lines up and fires.

"I tell yer boy, the bullet left a hole in the fog yer could put yer eye to, and look down a long dark tunnel where the slug had passed. We waits for a while and there's no more howls. "I reckon I got him", Steveo says. "I'll foller the bullet hole and find him".

He walks off inter the grey darkness, leavin' a bigger track than the bullet did. Just then a breeze comes and the fog starts to shift about. I becomes aware that me mate might get lost, so I gets a bullock bell and rings it. Pretty soon Stevo appears, draggin' the biggest dingo I ever saw. He points to the bullet's exit, a ragged bloody hole in the back of the dog's skull.

"I was right on target with his howl, mate", he says. "Got him through the roof of the mouth and out the back of the head. Wouldn't have got back without the bell to guide me".

"Sounds like Stevo had a radar in his head", I remarked.

"Not at all", Harry replied. "In those hard days blokes like me and Stevo had very little in our heads except the need for survival".

The Spirit Bullocks

"Demolition is an easy job to-day", I remarked to Uncle Harry. "The modern machines can knock down a building in a matter of minutes".

The old boy sucked hard on his pipe, eyeing me disdainfully as a stream of evil smoke filtered through his moustache.

"A good team of bullocks are just as effective", he claimed. "You have no idea my boy just how efficient they really are. I can recall when the entire front wall of a pub was demolished by a team of bullocks that was not even there".

"Come off it", I said. "You've been reading about radar machines".

"Not at all", Harry said severely. "Let me enlighten you. My old man, Bill Stapleford, was the beau-ideal of a bullock-driver. He could get 'em to turn handsprings in the yokes. Far and wide in the Maitland district his fame was known.

"Now just before he retired, an artist bloke from Sydney painted a portrait of the team, with Dad standin' beside Flint and Tinder, his two leaders. The landlord at a little bush pub bought the picture and hung it in the public bar near the entrance.

The years went by, and one day me and a few mates are standin' just across the road from the pub, yarnin'. There's a muffled shout from within the pub, then the whole front wall tears away from the rest of the buildin' and crashes inter the road, raisin' a big cloud of dust.

"We was all shocked as pigeons in a snake-pit. The blokes in the bar came staggerin' out, with the publican tryin' to gabble an explanation. "I dunno what caused", he gasps. "A bloke was lookin' at the portrait, and I tells him that its Bill Stapleford and his bullock team. Then just for fun I sings out "G'wup there!! G'wup Flint and Tinder-r-r!!"". Believe it or not, the leaders in the portrait hurls 'emselves inter the yoke, and the whole team follers. Down goes the wall".

"A likely yarn", I said scornfully.

"Not at all", Harry replied. "The old man's bullocks were long dead, but they were there in spirit. When the landlord called 'em up, they went at it and pulled the wall down. Spirits have been known to do strange things".

"The spirits that the publican was serving must have done strange things to certain blokes", I remarked darkly. "Thank the Lord modern demolition machines don't have spirits, only diesel fuel".

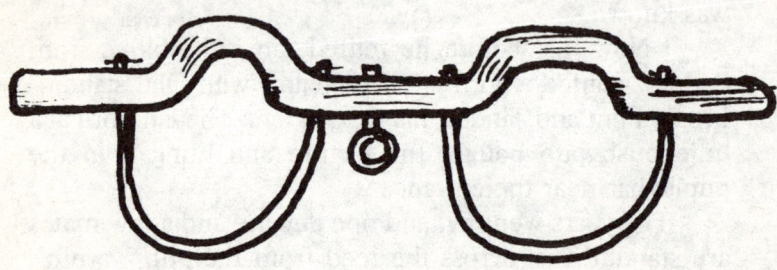

The Fish-God Worshipper

"The fish are off the bite", I remarked to Uncle Harry. "What it needs is a freshet in the river".

"Might make a difference", the old boy replied. "Yer hear a lot of tales about how to get 'em to bite, but I only saw one bloke with a foolproof system.

"Quite a few years ago it was, that I knew an old whaler, Queer Ned we used to call him. Always campin' in the river bends, and always had a string of fish hangin' from the tent-pole. Blokes used to wonder where he got 'em, and when they'd ask him he used to flash a silly grin, and tell 'em he used to offer up a special prayer to Dagon, the fish-tailed god of the ancient Phonecians. After that the fish used to bite. Nobody around the place had ever heard of this Dagon cove, so in their ignorance they labelled Queer Ned a lunatic. But they still couldn't work out how he got the fish.

"Ned always camped in lonely places, and came to town twice a week to sell fish. One day we notices he hasn't shown up for a while, so I decides to go and look for his camp. I knew his haunts pretty well, and sure enough I finds him in a big clump of river-gums, and believe it or not, he's laying' unconscious on his swag. I reckoned he's had a seizure of some sort, so I find a bottle of brandy in his tucker-box and gives him a big dose. He comes to life coughin' and splutterin', and lookin like as if he's been dead for a week. "Harry, old mate", he gasps, "I'm on me way. Get the oaken overcoat ready".

"You'll be right, Ned", I says. "I'm goin' for help".

He grabs me arm with surprisin' strength. "I'm done, Harry", he gasps. "Soon be fishin' in the river Styx. But before I go, I'll tell yer the secret of how to catch fish. Yer get a couple of dead rabbits and let the flies blow 'em, then hang 'em in a cage over a deep hole. The crows light on it tryin' to get at the rabbits, the cage shakes and the maggots drop inter the water. When this happens every day, the fish hang round waitin' for a feed. Then yer take the cage away and throw a line in. The fish are there waitin' to get hooked.''

In a flash I was made aware of how Ned was such a successful fisherman. I rises up to go for help, but he hangs on to me arm. ''Don't go yet, Harry'', he whispers. ''There's a point I haven't told yer about. Yer gotter.......''. His voice fades out and he falls down dead.

I went and got the local copper and the ambulance, and they took Ned for his last excursion, I couldn't wait to try Ned's trick for catchin' fish. Yer can't even imagine how disappointed I was when I couldn' get it to work. Tried it a dozen times without success.

''Can't see what was wrong'', I said.

''I know what was wrong'', Harry remarked sadly. ''Poor old Ned died before he could tell me''.

''I can't guess what that would be'', I said in a mystified voice.

''Yer pretty slow, boy'', Harry replied ''Poor Ned died before he could tell me the words of the prayer that yer gotter offer to Dagon, the fish-tailed god of the Phonecians. Without that the flyblown rabbits in the cage were like a rifle with no cartridges. But let's not grieve. Instead we'll go and thow a line in, and since we can't make contact with this Dagon character, we just gotter trust to luck''.

Force and Resistance

"I have often heard argument," I remarked to Uncle Harry, "regarding the result when the irresistable force meets the immovable object."

"There's no need for argument", Harry replied. "They both become losers".

"I remember a time when I worked for a wealthy bloke who was a crank on goats. Had quite a herd of 'em, and his pin-up goat was a cranky old billy called Charger. This was on account of he would charge anything that annoyed him. Nothin' could stand before him. He was the complete irresistable force.

"Now the bloke's wife was a crank on mirrors. Had 'em hung up everywhere, and in the lounge-room was a great big one set in the brick wall. About ten feet square, it was a bloody immense object, and really immovable.

"This bloke had no time for mirrors, and the wife hated goats, and this caused a lot of friction between 'em, and was finally the cause of a divorce. But I'm gettin' ahead of me story".

"One day the lady leaves the back door open, and in strolls Charger, accompanied be his latest love, a cute little nanny goat. They walks into the lounge, and Charger spots his reflection in the big mirror. He reckons it's a rival out to steal his nanny, and he starts to paw and snort. Of course, the reflection snorts and paws too, so Charger heads for the mirror full belt. The crash was like the clap of doom.

"When the damage was tabled, the goat had a broken neck and the mirror was smashed to flinders. So yer see, both were losers. The irresistable force was dead, and the immovable object was wrecked".

"What did the couple involved think of this?" I asked.

"The bloke claimed that the mirror was responsible for the death of the goat", Harry replied, "and the woman blamed the goat for the loss of the mirror. Anyhow they parted and were never reconciled. And it wasn't any irresistable force caused the dissolution. The trouble was, both of them, when it came to argument, were immovable objects''.

The Golden Opportunity

"A nice bit of mutton", said Uncle Harry, as he wiped the blade off his knife and looked happily at the dressed carcase of a fat stray sheep that had foolishly wandered into Harry's small flock of pets. "Now I'll tell yer somethin'. Never let a golden opportunity go past. Act quick as soon as it arises, because yer seldom get a second chance. And take no head of silly old platitudes that claim honesty is the best policy. God helps those who help themselves.

"I remember a cove who worked at Kookataterwell saleyards. We used to call him Magnet, because he had a habit of pickin' anything up. He ran a few black Angus cattle, and the day I recall he had eighteen of 'em in the sale, neat little two year old steers. One of the big stations had sent in a hundred and ten black Angus, all neat little two year old steers too. The agent was a bit of a new-chum, couldn't count real good. Him and Magnet counted 'em in. "Hundred and nine", says the agent.

"Should be a hundred and ten", says the ringer who drove the steers in. "What did you make it, Magnet?".

"A hundred and nine", says Magnet. "Bet on it".

"Must have been one of 'em got back off the camp last night", the ringer says. "They wuz pretty toey. Hundred and nine must be right if yer both made it the same".

"Bet on it", Magnet says. He didn't let on that he made the number one hundred and ten. He was a bloke who was always sure of his count.

"The ringer was satisfied, and makes off for the pub at a gallop, and the cattle were soon penned up. The agent goes off for his lunch, and anyone else there was too busy to take much notice of what's goin' on. Magnet quietly slips a steer out of the station lot, and puts it in his own pen of eighteen. Before long the sale kicks off and prices are good. They come to the pens of Angus cattle.

"A hundred and nine Angus steers", the agent says,

and they're sold pretty quick. On they go to Magnet's lot.

"Eighteen fine steers on account of Mr Magnet", the agent yells.

"Hold on, there's nineteen", Magnet yells. "I just checked 'em".

"Nineteen, buyers", the agent says, not suspectin' a thing wrong. They're gone in a few bids, bought be the same cove as bought the hundred and nine from the station. So when they all went in together the theft was foolproof. It was winter, and so long coats on the cattle made all brands indistinct. Nobody noticed the little steer that got himself duffed. Magnet hadn't missed the golden opportunity to get a free one.

"So yer see, boy", Harry concluded, "honesty isn't always the best policy, not from a financial point of view. And a man never should miss a golden opportunity".

The Joys of Bees' Nesting

In my boyhood my family lived a couple of miles from a small bush town. Just across the road lived the Stevens family, in which there were several boys around my age, and were close friends of ours. Their mother, Aunty Alice as she was known, was a formidable bush-bred lady who was prepared to tackle any job however difficult, including the robbing of bees' nests. Bush honey was quite a delicacy in those hard and hungry days of depression, and Aunty Alice and my mother decided to rob a nest situated in a dead box-tree about half a mile from our house. Careful preparations were made.

The two women led the party carrying the axe and pieces of mosquito-netting, while Art Stevens and yours truly brought up the rear, bearing buckets to hold the plundered spoil. behind us trailed Splinter, a mean and spiteful kangaroo-dog.

The bees seemed rather tame, and made no resistance as the women took turns on the axe. Mum could chop pretty well, as could most bush women of the time, but Aunty Alice was a female Leo Appo, and her powerful blows soon brought the old hollow tree tumbling to the ground. Our troops all made a hasty retreat as the bees swarmed out in clouds.

Splinter was our first casualty. Arthur threw a stick in among the fallen branches, and Splinter, thinking the boy had thrown at a rabbit, went forward to investigate. The howls and leaps he gave way to assured us that the bees were capable of a stubborn defence, but Aunty Alice was not at all daunted. After arranging the mosquito-net over her hat and in the collar of her dress to protect her face, she strolled calmly to the log and soon had a fire of bark going, which she covered with green bushes.

The bees were flabbergasted by the smoke and lost a good deal of their agressive attitude. The rest of us gained courage as Aunty Alice began to chop out the nest. Soon we were digging out long dripping slabs of honeycomb, quite unmindful of the odd sting received on our hands.

With out buckets full, we two boys began to eat the comb, despite Aunty Alice's dire warning that "it'll give you little buggers the belly ache". We chewed happily on, and my greed became my undoing.

A very large and hostile bee was buried in the honeycomb, and I unwittingly chose to crunch the portion in which this aggressive insect had chosen to make his last-ditch stand. When he stung me on the tongue the noise and convulsions I produced would have done credit to a scalded dog. I was finally seized and held down by mum, while Aunty Alice none too gently removed the embedded sting. Next day I was hardly able to talk, and had to live on liquids for a couple of days. Mum said the silence was wonderful, and more honeycomb should be eaten in hopes that more rebellious bees would keep children quiet.

The young people to-day don't bother to rob the bush nests. It is a lot easier and less fatiguing to buy honey at the supermarket. But as I look back on life, I can assure my readers that modern youth don't realise some of the delightful occupations they are missing.

The Hanging of Doug Doolin

In the little town where in the depression I spent my school days, there lived a character named Doug Doolin. He was Dublin born, and a returned soldier from the Kaiser's War, as the 1914 holocaust was always referred to by the locals.

Doug was a kind and harmless fellow, slightly shell-shocked. He lived in a tin shed at the back of the pub, and did odd jobs about the place. When in liquor he grew very despondent, and continually threatend to hang himself, but he always seemed to recover from his cups without carrying out the threat. he could be recognised night or day by the red-and-black striped Tiger Kelly sweater, which he always wore.

One night a bunch of schoolboys decided it was time Doug's threat was carried out. A very lifelike dummy was constructed from a pair of old dungaree trousers, worn Army boots, and an old straw hat like the one Doug always wore. It remained only to acquire the Tiger Kelly jumper.

Doug had been on the beer that afternoon, and after a careful reconnoitre, the door of his shed was opened. He was snoring peacefully, and was blissfully unaware of the removal of his jumper from a nail in the wall-plate.

The jumper really put the finishing touches on the effigy. The sinners agreed that it looked more like Doug than Doug did. A length of rope was acquired without the owner's consent, and "Bluey" Smith, who could climb like a trained goanna, shinnied up a telephone pole and hanged the dummy by the neck to a cross-bar. The boys then disappeared into the darkness to their respective homes.

Next morning at first light the jokers were all watching from strategic points. The chosen post was situated on a corner between the cafe and the butcher's shop, and Theo the Greek was the first to sight what he thought was Doug's corpse. He dropped his broom and headed for the police station, leaving his cafe to the mercy of the world. His yells could have been heard in Athens. "Oh, mine jasus! Doolin he been an' hang himself!".

A couple of women came round the corner, and on sighting the dummy, fled yelling "Oh my God. A man's been hung. It's Doug Doolin".

The news went round like a flash of lightning, and people came from all points of the compass. Soon a closer inspection revealed the fact that a dummy, not Doug, hung from the cross-bar. Constable MacAloon arrived, and became furious at sight of the hoax that had been perpetrated. He was an easy-going policeman, but didn't like being pulled out of bed for a foolish reason. Just at that moment the living Doug staggered up with a monumental hangover, threatening to "Kill the bludger who pinched me Tiger Kelly jumper".

"Can anybody climb up and get that thing down?" asked the constable.

"Bluey Smith is good at climbing telephone poles", some onlooker remarked.

MacAloon glared suspiciously at Bluey, but the boy's expression was an innocent as a baby rabbit's. "I want a shillin' to climb it", he said. "Mum goes crook if I climb poles".

MacAloon reluctantly handed over the shilling. He was Scotch by name as well as nature, but Bluey was adamant. On receiving the coin he scurried up and retrieved the dummy, and Doug, with much cursing got his jumper back. MacAloon threw the effigy in the back of his car and took it to the station, and by nightfall the prank was stale news. A month later Billy Francis was lumbered for drunkeness, and informed us on his release that the dummy was in the cell where he spent the night. Evidently Constable MacAloon meant to keep it where it couldn't cause any further disturbance.

Impromptu Rodeo

Holding impromptu rodeos with the town milkers was a favourite pastime in our little village. The teenagers of the depression didn't have bikes, social service and bop to amuse themselves. They were lucky if they got three feeds a day, so they had to make their own entertainment. I well recall one Saturday night when we set forth on a rough-riding escapade, several mischievous youths armed with a long rope, a blunt pair of spurs, and a surcingle. There was a dance in the local hall, but none of us had the price, so dancing was vetoed in favour of rough-riding.

We drove the cattle to a somewhat isolated yard on the edge of town, far enough way to avoid the unfavourable attentions of the local constable. There was a big red steer with the milkers, a straggler lost from a droving mob, and in due course he was captured and led out with surcingle attached. Darcy was our star rider, and he sprang aboard the steer, which was being held by the horns. On its release Darcy jabbed in the spurs, but the beast sulked and refused to move. Victor had brought along a cattle dog named Skipper, a canine colossus in his youth, but now gone slightly mad and blind from kicks received on the head.

"Sool him, Skipper", Vic ordered, and Skipper rushed in and grabbed the first thing his failing sight recorded, which was Darcy's boot. At that moment the steer took a flying leap forward, and Darcy, pulled off balance by the dog, went to grass quickly as the steer broke into a gallop.

Charlie and myself were holding the rope, and for once we were caught off guard, I stumbled and fell, and Charlie, a heavy Rugby star, fell on top of me. Away went the steer, heading down Chinaman's Lane with the rope attached. We knew that we had to get the rope and surcingle back, or we would be in trouble with the law next day. All hands set off through the moonlight in hot pur-

39

suit. Teddy and I were leading the field, but Bill, an even-time runner, soon went past us. Then all of a sudden he disappeared.

We didn't wait to see what had undone Bill, we had to catch that steer. Finally we cornered him and got hold of the rope. Bill came limping up, smeared with charcoal and ashes. He had fallen down a big hole where Shire workers had burned out a stump some days before. He was bruised but still game, and like the rest of us had regained confidence. Teddy was keen to have a ride but he was wearing his best clothes, having intended trying to gate-crash the dance. He only had one good outfit, (that was all any of us had in those days), and he couldn't afford to damage it. Suddenly an idea struck him. "I know", he said. "I'll ride in me underpants".

He stripped down to shoes, socks and briefs. We all gigged him, saying he must be representing a riding-team from a nudist colony.

The steer really bucked this time. Teddy made a terrific ride, and was finally thrown at a spot where the town cows were in the habit of camping. He made made a wild figure in the moonlight as he got up plastered with dust and cow-manure, but unhurt. We adjourned to a deserted farmhouse near-by, where he washed up at the tank with much friendly chiacking from his mates. But he was a happy soul, and was soon heading for the dance-hall while the rest of us departed to our respective homes.

It's really good to see young people to-day enjoying the current inflatory prosperity. But they don't enjoy life any more than the scruffy, penniless gang of which I was a member as a teenager. They are scattered now, and some have gone to their rewards, but if any of them read this little story I wish them all the best, and when I have my next beer, I will say here's Luck to the mates of my youth.

The Great Suntan Myth

In most places in our great country, Australians are believed to be a race of healthy, suntanned people. This belief is shared by a lot of folk from overseas. Gorgeous girls made a rich brown by the sun, and muscular Apollos cast in bronze, radiating faultless health. I can never understand why people undergo the agony of sunburn just for the sake of being tanned. In my book tans are strictly for the hide tanneries.

You see them in all coastal holiday resorts. Women who in my honest opinion become the most unfeminine type when roasted like boiled yabbies. Lobster red to near shades of black, with the skin peeling off them in flakes like a shedding tiger-snake, and their hair faded and dry as the mane of a brumby mare. And their faces smeared with a messy white concoction that causes them to resemble an American Indian on the warpath. Glamorous! Not on your life!

Then we have the male of the species. He is mostly a muscular moron, with a lot of the muscle inside his head. He seems to think his suntan gives him superiority over his fellows. I admit he is very impressive. That is until he makes conversation.

In my youth I worked in the harvest fields of the North-West on many occasions, so I do not have to be told that sunburn is one of the painful tortures that the human epidermis can endure. Yet many of my race suffer it in order to attain a colour that makes them quite as dark as an aboriginal, or nearly so. And when winter comes and clothes are donned, they are soon back to square one. I was once employed by a farmer who worked through the summer harvest attired in only boots and shorts, and was burned the colour of coal. He asked me where I was going to spend my holidays, and when I told him Kosciusko he almost fainted.

"Whadder yer make to that cold hole for", he asked

in disgust. "Why dontcher go to the Gold Coast where there's plenty of good sunshine". It was my turn to nearly faint.

I knew several sun-worshippers with tender skins and soft complexions who believed the sun's rays were the complete elixer of life. Even when treated for skin-cancers they refused to accept the fact that the sun was to blame. But they always wore shirts and long sleeves after a cure was affected.

Perhaps I am something of a drop-out for failing to conform with the great Australian Sunshine Myth. But I remember too well the days I spent in the harvest fields, and the endless miles I rode in the heat of summer on the plains, when I craved for the shade of an air-conditioned pub like a boozer craves for beer, away from the continuous annoyance of countless flies, ants, and mosquitoes as big as humming-birds.

No, gentle reader, I have no wish to expose myself to the sandflies and bluebottles that infest our beaches, and will quite happily remain a unhealthy, sickly-white Australian. Suntan is not for the Scribe from the Scrub.

Sense of Direction

"In the bush on a dark night", remarked Uncle Harry, "it's easy to lose yer sense of direction. A lot of thieves have got caught gettin' away from the scene of the crime, especially at night. They lose their sense of direction and dunno where they are".

"Has this ever happened to you?", I asked innocently.

Harry bristled. "Of course not, the reason being that I am an honest man. Up to a point, of course. But I recall a bloke named Joe Lifter, one of the biggest thieves I ever met. He was what yer call dedicated to dishonesty. Well do I remember the night he nearly got caught due to losin' his sense of direction. Only luck, and Stevo and me gave him.

"It was at a tank-sinkin' job out near Mungindi. We had Joe workin' on the scoop, and a good toiler he was. But his heart was in villianry. Always thinkin' up a lawless way to get rich quick, but he didn't have enough talent for major crime. Just a small-timer.

"One Saturday we finishes at dinner-time, intendin' to have the afternoon off. But not for Joe. He decides to take a walk in the bush, to see if he can pick up anything that isn't bolted down. Stevo and me watched him go, wonderin' if he's goin' to return or not.

"Darkness falls, and there's no sign of Joe. We sat up yarnin' until midnight, and he's still absent. "Most likely in the cooler, mate", Steveo says, and on that note we burrow up.

"Just daylight, we hears Joe comin'. Steveo had the fire blazin' and suddenly Joe appears with no trousers on, carrying a fat lamb over one shoulder with its legs tied, and two roosters, a bucket of eggs, and his strides in his spare hand. He's just on the point of collapse.

"Where the hell have yer been", I asks.

Joe drops his load and grabs a pint. He starts drinkin' tea like a famished camel. "I only went about two mile",

43

he says. "I spotted a house an watched it 'til I seen the people take off for town. I waited 'til nearly sundown, then goes and helps meself to the eggs and roosters. I'm on me way back when I comes on a mob of sheep with some prime lambs among 'em. I drops me plunder and takes off after 'em. Be the time I captures a lamb and ties him with me belt it's after dark. That's when me troubles started. I couldn't keep me trousers up without the belt, so I had to take 'em off and leave 'em with the sheep, while I go back for the fowls and eggs. I completely lost me sense of direction, and walked half the night before I found the plunder. And blast me luck, when I did find 'em, me sense of direction is still off target, and I searched 'til nearly mornin' before I found me strides and the sheep".

Joe gets in his swag and goes straight to sleep, while Steve and me butchered the sheep and fowls, and disposed of any incriminatin' evidence. We were none too soon, just as we finished a trooper rides up lookin' round very suspicious like, but he knew nothin' about Joe's misdeeds, and after he bludged a drink of tea he rode off. If he'd come an hour earlier it would've been a sweet fair cop. Joe nearly ended up in the bricks due to losin' his sense of direction".

"I wonder did he ever lose it again", I said.

"Dunno", Harry replied. "When he finished the job, we paid him off and he was never seen by us again. But Stevo found he was short of a new pair of moleskins, and I was missin' two shirts. Joe lost his sense of direction at times, but one thing he never lost was his sense of survival".

Bullswool the Rebel

In the long years that I knew him, Uncle Harry owned horses of many breeds and types. Racehorses, stock-horses, harness horses, not to mention ponies and draught animals. The one that I remember best was Bullswool, who was the epitome of equine villainy.

Harry acquired his unlovable creature for the sum of thirty-five shillings, at a public auction of animals impounded by the Shire Council. A stocky dark bay of fourteen hands with a sound and dependable appearance Bullswool, as Harry called him, was the supreme exponent of rebellion and refusal to co-operate.

He was not a bucker, oh no. Bullswool was too cunning to exhaust himself by any extreme physical effort. There were easier ways to thwart the many masters that he doubtless had before Harry got hold of him. To catch him was almost impossible. Harry would attach a heavy trace chain to a front fetlock, and Bullswool could not then gallop off. When caught he refused to lead and had to be dragged. When about to be saddled he could blow himself up like toad, so that the girth and surcingle were never tight. No amount of urging, cajoling or cursing could induce him to move. Only a sharp pair of spurs would put him off the mark, and at every chance he got he would swing off the track and do an about-face.

If there was only one tree in the paddock, Bullswool would hide behind it if he saw Harry approaching with a bridle, and when discovered would keep circling round his owner, staying just out of reach. Harry tried cattle dogs when all attempts to yard him failed, but the pony had a foolproof method for dealing with them. He would stand with one hind leg raised in readiness and when its opposite member was grabbed by the dog Bullswool would be watching with his head turned to the side. He at once delivered an effective kick with the raised hoof. Dogs with concussion, broken legs or dented ribs are of little use, so Harry decided that dogs were out of the question for Bullswool.

Harry attempted to lead him by tying him to the rear of the wagon, but the pony sat back hard and broke reins. A three-quarter inch rope was substituted for the bridle, and Bullswool was beaten, but only for a short time. While Harry was in the wayside pub taking a reviver, Bullswool chewed the rope in half and cleared off home, leaving his owner without a horse to muster the bullocks. Harry later replaced the rope with a chain, and the pony was forced to surrender. It was one of the few victories for the owner in the Harry vs Bullswool competitions.

On one occasion Bullswool entered the open door of the kitchen, drank all the milk that was in a bucket on the table, then availed himself of a freshly cooked damper. Two floor boards were broken as he made his escape. He survived this misdemeanor only because Harry couldn't find the gun-cartridges, and relented later.

Any gate with a sliding latch was a pushover for Bullswool, and Harry had to place chains and hooks on all gates to be sure they would remain shut. And how that pony loved rolling with the saddle if he could get free of rubbing the bridle off on a post. One day he got loose and went down to the dam, where he rolled in the mud after the saddle was saturated.

It was the last straw. Harry sold him to a passing drover, and two weeks later the old boy arose one morning to find Bullswool standing at the gate still wearing the remains of a bridle. He hadn't liked being away from Harry and home.

The drover came back later and collected him, while Harry stayed out of sight, fearing a refund of the purchase price would be requested. This time Bullswool went for good, and we never saw him again, though Harry oft lamented over this lost rebel, claiming that ''he'd of been a great pony if he hadn't been spoilt''.

But I doubt if lack of education and discipline, or wrong environment had anything to do with Bullswool's behaviour. Doubtless he was born to be what he was, despite maudlin excuses made by Uncle Harry.

The Card Players

My grandmother always claimed that cards were the devil's playtoys. A bigoted **minister** told me that cards are the paving stones on the path to ruin. A barmaid I was rather fond of informed me that playing cards would keep me broke always. This seemed strange, as she was devoted to poker-machines. A rather unenlightened old gentleman, (Who was a left-over from the gaslight era) bombarded me with stern admonishments, saying that shame and poverty lay in a pack of cards. But despite all these dreadful warnings, I always enjoy a game with the paste-boards.

In the Depression, card-playing was a great pastime in my home town. There was seldom money involved, as the residents were most of the time pennliness. But all kinds of games were played with a feverish interest produced by boredom. My father was card-shark of repute, and he educated me in the arts of euchre and five-hundred at a very early age.

The verandah of Mr Budda Deen's home on Bingara Street was a great gathering for the card-players. Budda Deen was a very respected gentleman from Pakistan who greatly enjoyed a game, as did Abdul Guffer, a rascally little Moslem. Both men had been in Australia a long time, earning a living as hawkers. One day they challenged Dad and I to a game of five-hundred just for the fun of it, as all hands were short of cash. I distinctly remember one hand that was played.

Budda Deen dealt, and the first bid was Dad's. He called nine-no trumps. I immediately realised that he held the Joker. To call nine without the top card was suicidal. I was stunned when Abdul, who had the next bid, called ten-no trumps. That quickly finished the Pakistani partnership. For Dad knocked off Abdul's lead with the Joker, and that was that. Budda Deen arose with a look of hopeless disgust on his face, and announced.....

"What the hell you doin', Guffer?. You musta know Dick hava the Joker or he not go the nine".

Abdul's reply was a stunner. "I not think Dick hava the Joker, Budda Deen. I thinka the boy have it".

I simply couldn't follow Abdul's reasoning, for I held the Joker and it was just as lethal in my hand as in my partner's.

Budda Deen's disgust was now so heavy that a hydraulic jack wouldn't have lifted it. "You wanta go back to the bloody Bombay, Guffer", he said sadly. "You got the no chance in Australia".

Euchre parties were often held on Saturday nights, at the home of anybody who liked to organize them. One shilling was the fee to enter, the prize being some simple gift costing around two-and-six. Any spare cash went to some charity or other. Strong drink was taboo, and good behaviour was the order of the night. At the conclusion there was tea and cake, plus social gossip. Next day tables and chairs were returned, having been borrowed for the event, to be borrowed again the following Saturday.

During wet weather in the shearing-sheds, I have more than once watched shearers and shed-hands play cards all night. The popular games were euchre, pontoon, five-hundred, poker and rummy. On droving camps I have often played until late into the night with the camp-fire the only illuminant. I knew one family who cut cards to see who did the hard part of the housework, low card losing, and in bush pubs cards were played continuously for drinks. But alas, those days are gone.

A flush of money (and dole) for the people, plus T.V., mini-pool and other mechanised amusements, plus that great trap the poker-machine, have put card-playing out of vogue. Also the youth of to-day have neither the sense or the inclination to learn how. But I feel that card-playing, when money is not involved, is one of the most educational and inexpensive pastimes that young people can indulge in, for it requires patience and mental concentration. But of course, I am old fashioned. Bring on the latest dirty, unkempt, mindless, barefoot pop-star, please gentlemen. He will supply our youth of to-day with all the brain-food necessary to help them succeed in to-days permissive, socialistic, corrupt and decadent world.

Exit Quinyan

The common possum, referred to by the aborigines of North-Western New South Wales as "Quinyan", is becoming alarmingly scarce. Not so long ago they were in countless numbers along the far-inland rivers. All night their chattering could be heard in the gums, and every hollow stump and log was filled with their kidney-shaped pellets of dung. Though in the main nocturnal creatures, they could be seen sleeping in the forks of trees on hot days.

But not any more. Quinyan is now in drastically reduced numbers, and little sign of him can be found in his old habitats. Something has been responsible for his quick disappearance. But what?

Purplish-grey in colour, with a light creamy under-belly, the female differs little in appearance from the male, except that the latter wears two brick red shoulder-patches. With small erect black ears, big luminous eyes and a long, dainty pink nose, Quinyan is one of Australia's most endearing marsupials. Not as quaint as the koala, but much more lovable.

Two bucks battling for the favours of an amorous female provide a contest more humourous than brutal. They punch, scratch, bite and wrestle, but put much greater effort into screeching than fighting. The loser usually retires quickly to a high bough, where he hurls abuse at the victor, while the bone of contention waits coyly in a hollow spout or a clump of mistletoe. Some weeks later (I do not know how long the gestation period is), the female will be seen on a horizontal branch with junior crouched on her back like Tod Sloan. How old he is when he vacates the pouch is also beyond the knowledge of a layman.

Quinyan makes an adorable pet, and will eat almost any food offered. Unfortunately he can never be house-broken, and performs his natural functions from the walls and rafters, causing consternation to the tidy and hygenic housekeeper.

The early Depression years saw a reduction in the possum population, when government declared an open season, and the marsupials were killed for their skins. Favourite bait of the hunters were pellets containing a mixture of treacle, rolled oats, oil of rhodium and wintergreen. To this cyanide was added. Often two quinyans were found dead beside the same bait, proving that a brain-poison strikes quickly.

Depression days also saw Quinyan on many a poor family's table, grilled, or roasted and stuffed with onions and herbs. When cooked, the flesh is as tender and white as that of a fowl, and exhudes a faint eucalyptus flavour. But the people in those hard times were hungry, and as one old bushman remarked to me "Eucalyptus is a medicine anyway." So Quinyan did his bit for the 1930's unofficial Freedom From Hunger Campaign.

But Quinyan is passing. Not one fifth of his countless numbers survive on the western streams to-day. Old bushmen claim that myxomatosis, released to destroy the rabbits, also wiped out the quinyans. Landholders and scientific boffins become enraged at this suggestion, but I often wonder, for the quinyans disappeared at the same time as bunny. Blame is also laid on the distribution of 10-80 poison, and I myself have seen dead quinyans in the wake of the poisoners. But no investigations have ever been made, so who rightly knows?

Very few present-day Aussies are interested in our native fauna and its survival chances. Progress thunders on, and mankind becomes more and more susceptible to the deadly and contagious disease called greed. Quinyan may hang on for a long time yet, but one day his extinction will be final. Unless the human race exterminates itself first with a big nuclear bang.

A Tale of Two Fish

"Fish", said Uncle Harry, "can be diabolically clever. It's a mistake to think that fish have a brain the size of a peanut".

"I know quite a few two-legged creatures who get by with less". I said.

"Be that as it may", the old boy replied. "But there is no fish as brainy as the Barwon Cod. And I speak from experience.

"Once I was fishin' on the Barwon out near Bourke, and believe me boy, they were bitin' well. I'm just fillin' me pipe when I chances to look up river, and fifty yards away I sees a big Cod jumpin' out of the water and fallin' back. Up he would go, then splasho. Back in the water. I walks up to where he was performin', baits a line and throws it in with hopes of catchin' him.

"When I go back to me possie, the bait-can is missin'. A bloody funny happenin', believe me. Not a sign of it anywhere.

"I went to me camp and dug some more bait, got a new can, and next day I'm back fishin'. I'm not there long before I see the big cod jumpin' again. I heads off to set another line for him, then finds I've forgot to bait the hook. I turns back, and for a moment I thought I was seein' things. Here's a great big cod out on the bank, and he's makin' for the water with bait-can in his mouth!

"I gives a yell and he drops the tin, then take a leap for the water. I hit him with a flyin' tackle, and he struggled like mad until I overpowered him. If ever a fish had a disgusted look in his eye, that one had. I woke up then what his lurk had been. His mate, or accomplice if yer wish, used to jump out of the water to draw me attention, and as soon as me back was turned he'd hop out and grab the bait-can. A strategic operation by two clever fish".

"You never saw his mate again?" I queried.

"No boy", Harry said sadly. "I wish I could have caught him too. He must have took off for distant places, realisin' that human brains are superior to those of a fish".

Mutton for Kings Cross

"Yer know", I said Uncle Harry, as he scraped the dead nuclear fall-out from his evil pipe," some people dunno good meat when they eat it. And others, especially city people, can eat meat of any sort and not know if it's good or bad, or what the hell the animal was that if came off".

I ran off an extra large slice from the rump I was carving, and deposited it on Harry's plate. "Have a go at that", I said. "And if you want an argument, tell me it's not good".

"I know it's good", the old boy replied as he fastened his two remaining teeth in the proffered tit-bit. "I can always tells good quality meat. But some blokes dunno the good from bad.

I remember a time when me and Steveo were sinkin' a tank near Gunnedah. The squatter we were workin' for was a real good cove, told us to yard the killers and knock one any time we needed meat.

"Now there was a friend of the boss, up from Kings Cross on a visit. He was an income-tax investigator, so he rated pretty low with Stevo and me. Also he was an authority on every bloody thing. A real noxious know-all. One day the boss comes down and asks us to kill a sheep for the city visitor. He was goin' back to Sydney, and wanted it for his family and friends. Bit of a social lion, he was. Or so it appeared. We agreed, makin' reservations about the kind of sheep we had in mind.

"We runs the mob in, and settles on a big, hard old ram about ten years old, with wrinkles on his neck and tail-butt like the armour on a mediaeval knight. We decides he's just the thing to strengthen the jaw-muscles of Sydney high society, so we grabs him. He looked so tough that even the knife-blade was shakin' with doubt. But with a tremendous physical effort requirin' great strength, Stevo cut his throat.

"We took turns at skinnin', and at last, with both of us on the verge of complete exhaustion, and every knife in the camp blunt, we gets the hide off.

We rose early next mornin' and cuts rammo in two with the cross-cut saw. Stevo nearly had a heart attack cuttin' him into chops. And we gets him packed in a box just as the sun was risin'. And let me tell yer, boy that mutton smelled ranker than a dingo den. Along comes the city boy in his car and collects the box. "My word", he says, "this meat has a delightful aroma. The flavour should be excellent".

"We could see he fair-dinkum meant it, so his remark took the wind out of our sails quite a lot. Off he goes headin' for the smoke, and we're happy to see the back of him.

"A month goes by, and one day the boss tells us that the city boy is back on another visit. That afternoon he lands at our camp all smiles and handshakes. "I'm terribly grateful to you men for killing me that lovely sheep", he tells us. "We held an outdoor party, and all our exclusive guests agreed that the country mutton was by far the tastiest thing served. You must kill me another one like it before I go home".

"That really stonkered us, we were too flabby-gasted to speak, and when the conny-sewer of meat goes off, Steve throws me a silly grin. "I think we better open a butcher's shop in Sydney, mate", he says. "We're in the wrong game".

"I had to agree, but I reckoned if I ever need false teeth, I'll go to Kings Cross to get 'em made".

A Discourse on Shed Rouseabouts

"The modern-day rouseabout", said Uncle Harry, "Is not very energetic and agile. He is too well fed, and works much shorter hours than he should. These and other benefits tend to make him lazy and sloppy".

"I would argue on that", I replied. "Not long ago I saw a young bloke do the whole board for six shearers, sweep as well as pick-up".

"Nothing amazing about that", Harry said. "I once picked-up and swept for ten, and the bloke on the chain was doin' a hundred and eighty. Most of me time was spent fillin' me pipe. I used to stand the broom on its end at number one stand, run down the board to number ten and pick the fleece up, and was back at the wool-table in time to grab the broom before it fell to the floor. I didn't do it often, as the boss may have thought I was lairising.

"Another feat for which I was noted was carried out in the hut on goin' to bed. I could blow out the kerosene lamp and jump into bed before the room got dark. Sometimes the bed was twelve feet from the lamp and this made the feat slightly difficult. Also I was never happy when it rained. I was so full of energy that laying round the hut all day was terribly boring. Consistent rain makes rouseabouts indolent and overweight.

"I once knew a rousie who claimed he could bring rain by praying. No contractor would employ him. At last he got a job, and he prayed for rain every night. Dry weather continued for weeks. That contractor wouldn't have lost him for the world. But the squatters reckoned he was causin' a drought and asked him to stop his prayers for rain. The moment he did, down came the rain in torrents. So yer see boy, it doesn't do to put much faith in prayer".

"Not when the rousies offer it', I said. "And you never hear of shearers praying".

"Of course not", Harry agreed. "They're so busy drinkin' and shearin' that they haven't time for prayer.

Anyhow, the only God they worship is Jack Hennessy''.

"Do you think they ever build hopes of the future?" I asked. "Yes", replied Harry. "Their hopes of the future are a quick cut out and a safe journey to the nearest pub, where they will worship their God Jack Hennessy''.

"And what do the rouseabouts worship?," I queried.

"Hard to say", Harry replied thoughtfully. "But take the old-time squatters who employed the shearers and rousies. They didn't have to worship anyone. They always had things made for 'em".

Ulterior Motive

"In this bloody crazy world of ours", said Uncle Harry, "Yer always gotter be on guard against confidence men. Blokes who when yer in trouble will lead yer to safety, then take yer for all yer got after. Lawyers and barristers are the same".

"Men with ulterior motives", I commented.

"Too right", the old boy replied as he fired up his foul fumigator. "And it's common to creatures other than human, too. I remember a time when I was fishin' on the Gwydir, east of Moree. There was a bit of an island in the middle of the river, and all around it was low-lyin' swampy country. There must have been rain up on the watershed, because the river started to rise pretty quick. Soon the ground was two inches deep in water, and along the edge comes a colony of mice, lookin' to get to the safety of the island. But the stream, though only about six feet wide was too deep for the mice to swim it. They were squeakin' with fear and runnin' up and down the edge, not knowin' what to do. They looked like gettin' drowned, when the water got a bit higher. One old feller was down on his knees with his paws clasped, makin' awful noises, and I reckoned he was prayin' to whatever gods mice believe in.

"Just when all seemed lost, a big carpet snake appears. He was a real stunner about ten feet long. He winds the end of his tail round a reed that was growin' on the water's edge, then swims across and grabs a root on the other side with his teeth, so that his body forms a bridge. The mice woke up quick and scampered across to safety, and the old snake let's go his tail hold and follers 'em. How d'yer like that?"

"That snake must have been a real Christian reptile", I said very doubtfully.

"That's where yer right off the track", Harry replied. "I went back a week later, and the water was still pretty high. That old snake was asleep on the island, sunnin' himself. He was shinin' fat and overweight, full and contented. And there was no sign of any mice, as I already said.

"What happened to them?", I asked.

"That old serpent was really clever", Harry continued. "I woke up to his dodge. He helped the mice over to the island, knowin' that once there they couldn't escape. Then he ate 'em up at his leisure".

"So yer see, boy, it doesn't do to put too much trust in a bloke who does yer a good turn. Two legged reptiles, worse than the carpet species. They'll lead yer to destruction with a false smile and a disarmin' manner, with what seems at the time a Christian act, But it's really an ulterior motive".

Death of a Traitor

"The best days of a bloke's life are his school days", remarked Uncle Harry. "But we don't realise it at the time. I Often wish I could go back and never leave".

"Of course you must have been a well behaved pupil", I suggested.

Harry took a long pull at his toxic pipe. "Well no, not exactly", he admitted. "I was a bit of a rebel. So was me mate Mick, the boy who lived next door. The teacher at our little bush school we attended was a tough old Scot named McKane. We used to call him Muchcane. Behind his back, of course. He used to do a lot of wardrobe drinkin' on week-ends. Teachers in those days were not supposed to set the kids a bad example, so their sins were committed away from the public eye. We had to be on our best behaviour Monday mornings, because Muchcane would be cranky with a hangover as big as Ayer's Rock.

"One hot Monday mornin' he's givin' us a lesson in English History. We never got any Australian History, just like we got Kipling's Poems and not Henry Lawson's. Cheers for our mighty British Empire, by Gad sir!! Anyway it's as hot as Hell's hinges, and there's a lot of blow-flies buzzin' around. Old Muchcane is soundin' off about Charles the First".

"When Charles was beheaded", he tells us, "the executioner held up the dead king's head and said "This is the head of a traitor".

"Out of the corner of me eye I sees Mick's hand flash out and grab a blow-fly. Like lightnin' he nips its head off with his pocket-knife and then holds the head up on the blade. "Get on this, Harry", he whispers. "This is the head of a traitor".

"I bursts out laughin' like a hyena, couldn't help meself. Next minute I'm hauled out in front of the class'.

"What were you laughing at?", old Muchcane asks.

"Nothin' sir", I says, shiverin' in me boots.

"Nothing, eh", he says. "Well I'll give you something to laugh at".

"Mick puts his hand up. "Please sir, it's my fault", he says. "I cut a blow-fly's head off and reckoned it was the head of traitor".

"Old Muchcane eyed us off and then starts to grin. "Go and sit down", he says. "You must have been paying me some attention".

"Harry lit his pipe and drew heavily as he concluded. "That was the only occasion, boy, when I ever saw old Muchcane show any mercy. Somethin' he didn't have was a sense of humour".

Just a Little Fish

"It's a very hard thing", said Uncle Harry, "to judge the size of a fish while he's still in the water. The river keeps many secrets".

"Would be next door to impossible", I said. "He'd have to be out on the bank or on the surface".

Harry baited his hook, then filled his pipe thoughtfully. "I was once completely fooled by a fish", he said. "Thought it was much smaller than it really was. For a moment when I had him hooked, I thought that I had at least caught the one that always got away".

"There was a big storm up on the watershed, and the river rose in a matter of hours. The muddy water was so thick that the fish were sick and surfacin', as you've seen 'em do at odd times. Stevo and me grabs our gaffs and hikes down the stream, which is runnin' strong a hundred yards wide. We decides to split up and take a side each, keepin' pace with each other, with the stream between us.

"I hooked a few little fellers out, then I notices a fish's nose stickin' out of the water. Like a flash I drives the gaff into it, and finds I'm really on to somethin' big. Pull as I might I can't move him.

"I hears a yell from Stevo, and lookin' across I sees he's got a fish be the tail, but he's in the same boat as me, can't drag him out. I'm haulin' for dear life, and so is Stevo on the opposite bank a hundred yards away. All of a sudden me gaff tears out of the fish's nose, and Stevo starts gainin' ground, slowly haulin' his fish up the bank. Then luck deserts him and his gaff tears out too. We looks at one another across that stretch of muddy water, and it slowly dawns on us what happened".

Harry paused to make a dramatic gesture with his pipe, while I waited impatiently. "Come on", I said. "The suspense is awful".

"The fact is", the old boy concluded, "is that Stevo and me had both gaffed the same fish. I had him by the

61

nose, and on the opposite bank a hundred yards away, Stevo had him by the tail. We were haulin' against each other".

"A fish a hundred yards long", I said incredulously. "Impossible".

"Not at all", Harry replied. "Who can see what's under the water? As I told yer earlier, the river holds many secrets".

Dingo Dissention

"There's a lot of dissention and strife in the world to-day", I remarked. "What's wrong with the system?"

"The system is alright", Uncle Harry replied. "It's the people who cause dissention.

"I was talking to a bloke at the pub", I said. "He reckoned a socialistic government would end the world's troubles".

"Of course he would be a successful man", Harry said. "A man with ambition, skill and brains".

"No, he wasn't I replied. "He was a cadger who never worked in his life. Existed on the dole".

Harry flashed a cunning grin. "I will tell you a fairy story, me lad", he said. "As a rule I don't specialise in fairy tales, but this one will give you food for thought when socialists bash your lug".

I herewith relate Uncle Harry's tale, presented in my own style.

* * * * * *

Once upon a time there lived in a deep bush a pack of dingoes, and there was one cleverer than all the rest. He visualised a better system to benefit the pack. He had nine cunning friends, and he sent them to call the pack together for a meeting. The pack was composed of a large percentage of Underprivileged Dingoes, a small percentage of Ambitious Dingoes, and of course the Clever Dingo and his Nine Friends.

"I have a plan called Betterment for Dingoes", he said. "I will be your leader, with my nine friends being the Governing Committee". (He was the originator of "Jobs for the Boys").

Every dog applauded, because was he not the Clever Dingo? and so his scheme was quickly adopted.

"There must be a fair share for all", he announced. "We cannot allow some to grow rich while others remain poor. Where is the Leading Lifter of Lambs?"

The Leading Lifter of Lambs stepped forward, a huge and powerful dog made muscular by much physical effort.

"How many lambs did you lift to-day?", asked the Clever Dingo.

"Eleven", was the reply.

"You will immediately give ten to the Governing Committee" ordered the Clever Dingo. "One you may keep for your efforts, but you must accept the fact that heavy taxes are required to establish the new system. Now you and the minority group can go and lift some more lambs for the Underprivileged Dingoes, as they are unfortunate."

The Leading Lamb Lifter was not at all pleased with these orders but he had voted to accept the Committee and its laws, so he went off with his hard-working minority to lift more lambs.

The Clever Dingo surveyed his people. "Where", he asked, "is the Superior Snitcher of Bitches?"

The Superior Snitcher stood up. He was a tall dark and handsome dog, with a winning personality that made bitch snitching easy.

"How many bitches did you snitch last night?" asked the Clever Dingo.

"Fifteen", said the Snitcher. "All high class kelpies from the stations. Sleek and hard-working".

That is what we need", said the Clever Dingo. "Hard workers, so that the committee can levy taxes to support our new system, and make sure that the Under-privileged Dingoes receive enough benefits. You will at once turn over these fifteen bitches to the Committee. You will be required to snitch a few more for the Under-privileged Dingoes, so they can work at populating the community. They cannot be expected to do anything else, because they are unfortunate creatures".

The Snitcher wasn't at all happy about this arrange-ment, but he had supported the Committee rules, so off he went with his minority group to do a bit more snitch-ing.

Time went by, and the Committee and the Under-privileged Dingoes grew fat and contented while the minority group hunted and snitched until they were sore-footed and disgusted. They held a secret meeting.

Revolution was suggested, but the minority soon were made aware by it's more intelligent members that they had not sufficient numbers to carry an insurrection. The committee had grown strong by supplying jobs for the boys, and giving the Underpriviledged Dingoes large quantities of lifted lambs and snitched bitches. These latter dingoes were increasing in alarming numbers, and the Minority Dingoes were required to lift and snitch harder than ever to help these unfortunates.

The Clever Dingo made long flattering speeches, claiming that the Committee was building a supreme culture, and soon the pack would be too strong for creatures to invade and conquer, and prosperity would be established for all time. But the Minority Dingoes grew angry and sullen, and did not lift and snitch to the full extent of their ability, and soon the pack was on the verge of famine.

"You must do more lifting and snitching", said the Clever Dingo. "How do you expect the Committee to function properly if it is denied its fair share of the system's benefits. Also the Underprivileged Dingoes are entitled to share with the rest. They cannot be expected to lift and snitch, because they are underprivileged".

The Leading Lamb Lifter was about to argue the toss when a motor was heard, and a truck appeared, driven by a Human. On the back of the truck were several dead lambs and a couple of scrawny kelpie bitches. The Human dropped his cargo and drove off.

"See!" said the Clever Dingo. "The Humans have recognised our superior culture and are prepared to give us lambs and bitches. The Committee will take these gifts, and the rest of the pack can wait for the next delivery to arrive".

The Underprivileged Dingoes all laid down and waited for the truck to return, but the Minority Dingoes

65

went off to lift and snitch, as they considered that accepting charity was degrading to strong and able dingoes.

Next morning they returned to find the Committee all dead, for the Human had poisoned the carcases of the lambs.

The Leading Lamb Lifter took charge. "We have fallen victims to our own ineptitude", he said. "Due to inactivity on the part of our majority, we are close to starvation. We will be easy prey for the Humans and their superior culture. We will go far into the deep bush and form a new colony".

The Underprivileged Dingoes were very frightened. "What will WE do", they howled.

"You may join us", said the new leader. "But you must earn your privileges like the rest of us. And the Governing Committee will have to lift and snitch too. No more free loading".

Far in the bush they formed a new colony, where every dog pulled his weight and was soon independent, due to personal enterprise".

★ ★ ★ ★ ★ ★

"Does your yarn insinuate that socialism would not be a success", I asked Uncle Harry.

"You be the judge, boy", Harry replied craftily.

★ ★ ★ ★ ★ ★

66

A Discourse on Water

Uncle Harry was in a talkative mood as we sat down to eat smoko. It was a typical harvest day, "hot as the hinges on the gates of hell", as the old boy described it. No amount of water seemed to quench our thirsts.

"Different waterholes in the bush have different types of water", Harry began. "Stevo and me once camped by a lagoon that was so full of salt and minerals that we submerged a dressed sheep in it. When we pulled him out next morning he was perfectly pickled like a well-cured ham".

"How did you get on for a drink?", I asked.

"The water-drums on the wagons were full of rain-water", Harry replied. "Luckily there was a heavy dew that night, and it left the blacksoil a waterlogged mess. When it melted there was enough water in the ruts for the bullocks to have a drink.

"I also recall a waterhole that must have been full of tasty vitamins and tonics. We unyoked on dark, and the bullocks were back and forwards all night, drinkin' this magic elixer. Next day we did a ten mile stretch to water. The bullocks were dog tired, but they still walked back ten miles to the liquid that contained the vitamins and cetra.

"Was there a pub nearby?", I asked innocently.

"There was, it was only half a mile from the waterhole", Harry informed me.

"Are you sure that you and Stevo didn't go back ten miles for some liquid with vitamins in it?", I queried.

"I dislike insinuating remarks", Harry replied. "We were discussing waterholes, remember. There was a lonely hole up near Ashford that was always warm even in winter. I dived in it one day, and the deeper I went the hotter the water became until I had to surface".

"Wonder what caused it", I said.

"The solution is quite simple", Harry said. "The roof of Hell was the bottom of the hole. When Old Nick

67

stokes the fires up for a few incomin' sinners, the water up above nearly boiled''.

"Your tale is taking a religious trend", I said. "Or possibly a scientific one''.

"Not at all", Harry replied. "I'm not religious or scientific. I'm simply truthful and practical. The young Australians of to-day are not truthful or practical. They have no wish to be. They believe anything that they wish to believe. That's why so many of 'em are on the dole''.

Revenge is Costly

"People tell yer that revenge is sweet, but it can be bloody costly too", remarked Uncle Harry. "And blokes who seek revenge often become the instrument of their own destruction".

"You sound as if you have seen this proved, old uncle", I replied.

"On more than one occasion", Harry replied dogmatically." I remember best a happening in the Monaro hills, a few years ago.

"There was a bloke had a cattle property. He was known as Hungry Hector, because he wasn't very open-handed or forgivin', and he caught the local poundkeeper duffin' a couple of his cows.

"Hungry had a bit of pull with the P.P. Board and the Shire, and he got the poundkeeper the sack. As yer know, poundkeepers are noxious insects, and this one, who was known as Bludger Bill, was a real scoundrel. His mother loved him for a little while when he was small, but nobody ever did after. He decided to take revenge on Hungry Hector.

"Hungry's stud cow paddock was on a steep hill near the highway, and the semi-trailers used to come down it like bullets. Bludger Bill decided to go out one moonlight night and stampede Hungry's cows out on to the highway when a semi was comin', and get a few of 'em killed by impact. A real dastardly scheme.

"Bill goes down in the night and opens the gate, then ties his horse up outside and sneaks round the cows on foot, takin' a white sheet with him. He pokes the cows up to the gate quietly, then waits 'til he sees the lights of a semi comin' down the hill. Then he rushes at the cows, wavin' the white sheet. But his plan misfired, because the cows didn't co-operate. They broke and scattered, takin' no heed of the open gate. Then things really went bad for Bludger Bill".

Harry paused to light his pipe, and I waited impatiently for him to resume. "Come on", I said. "The suspense is unbearable".

Harry puffed and grinned. "Bill's horse was a bit toey, and when it saw the sheet flappin' it pulled away, and goes gallopin' inter the road right in the path of the semi. The driver goes for the brakes, but too late.

"There was an awful crunchin' noise, and Bill's horse is transformed into somethin' very close to mincemeat. The saddle, an expensive one, is a complete write off, and worse is to come later. The truckie took legal action, and Bill had to pay a big account for damages to the semi.

"So yer see, revenge is not always sweet. It can be bitter, and worse than that, bloody costly".

Old Bush Superstitions

I have never in any way been superstitious, which is remarkable when I consider countless unfound beliefs that plagued the people of my home town. Probably most of these childish superstitions originated back in the dark ages, and were handed down from one generation to the next. But there are others involving flora and fauna that must have had their origin since the arrival of Captain Cook.

By many people the bite of the Australian ring-snake or "bandy-bandy" is considered to be more dangerous than that of the taipan. Believers claim that symptoms take the form of violent fits, one for each black band on the reptile's body. But scientists have proved that this small pied serpent is non-venomous.

One old bushman of my acquaintance claimed that goanna-oil applied to any part of the human body would cause the bones to decay. When asked why the aboriginals used it without mishap, he grinned wisely and announced that" it oney affects white bones. Evidently he believed that an abo's bones are the same colour as his skin.

An old fisherman I knew would never break a bough from a willow tree. He always claimed that to break willow was the unluckiest act possible. There was also a bush-worker who would never begin a job on Friday, as this was sure to herald dire mishap. And to cut a child's hair before it was a year old was to invite its death.

There was a transient family who would never shift a broom from one camp to another. They were always moving round leaving a new broom behind. They claimed that shifting a broom always swept away their good luck. None of them had any success in life. Another of their reversed superstitions was never to kill a cat. This produced bad luck of the worst type.

There was a lady who claimed she could tell the sex of an unborn child by rubbing the pregnant mother's wedding ring. I noticed that she never disclosed her diagnosis until after the child was born. I don't know how she got on with the numerous children that were born out of wedlock.

It was also considered very unlucky to count the cars following a funeral. To kill a cricket was to invite the utmost bad fortune. Chinamen were considered the greatest harbingers of good luck. To acquire "the luck of a Chinaman" was paramount to all other gifts from the gods. Anybody who suffered from nervous disorders was believed to have "killed a Chinaman".

To keep a tooth after extraction was a terrible taboo, as superstition argued that a canine fang or "dog's tooth" would grow in its place.

I could continue forever in this vane, just as the old beliefs will continue in the minds of semi-literate outback people. But then I must remember that the average Australian is pretty gullible. You only have heed the way that we take notice of our politician's promises to realise that.

Needlecraft in the Bush
(A Dying Art)

In these days of inflated prosperity, patched clothes are seldom seen in the outback, a clear contrast to the days of depression, when the garments of the bushworker were predominantly a forest of patches growing together. It was the era of the skilled seamstress, and women who could not sew were regarded as white cargo in any home in the bush occupied by working people. Money was a scarce commodity, and skirts and pants were patched and re-patched, often with greatly contrasting materials and colours. I have seen pieces of canvas from a worn-out waterbag used to patch the knees of a shearer's dungaree trousers.

The backs of trouser-legs always copped the least wear and tear, and these were cut from the hopelessly worn-out garment, and used to patch the seat of a pair somewhat better. Shirt-tails were also used to repair tears and holes.

Flour could be bought in fifty-pound bags, and the bag when empty would have holes cut for the arms and head to go through, and hemmed neatly. Result, a handy summer shirt, bearing across the back the insignia, "Brunton's Quality Flour". (Upside down). The twenty-five size fitted small children.

Old threadbare blankets were sewn together and covered with cheap cretonne, thus producing the bushman's "wagga", a bedcover for the winter. "Wagga" could also be slept on in the summer. Washing this cumbersome quilt could be an ordeal, but bushwomen were tough and tenacious.

Wool-bales filched from a shearing-shed were cut to bed size and covered for waggas, and the cap from the bale supplied many shearers with working footwear. I recall an aboriginal "gun" shearer called Leo Raveneau who was an artist in the construction of the bag mocassin.

73

Leo would fashion the slippers with turned up toes like the boots of a Killarney goblin, cutting them with the shears and sewing dainty stitches with twine.

Many hours were spent in the evenings darning socks, a forgotten and obselete profession today. Television was non-existent, and reading material was scarce.

Flannel was always kept in good wearing order, as it was an unshakeable belief among bush people that this material was a sure protection against all chest complaints. When shearing I suffered continually with chest complaints until I discarded flannels, and I have seen old fellows who wore them all their lives coughing their lungs out with consumption.

The women wore patches too, mostly on skirts and aprons, and there were patchwork quilts of all types, sizes and colours. Many women bought cheap calico and made their own sheets and pillowslips.

The Afghan camel drivers practiced a barbaric form of needlecraft. Reach for the smelling salts please, all members of the R.S.P.C.A. You are in for a shock! When a camel developed a sore or gall, a piece of canvas was placed over the injury and SEWN TO THE SKIN OF THE LIVING ANIMAL. So much for animal liberation in those hard days.

Prosperity, and mass production of cheap garments made of plastic and nylon, (not to mention synthetic wool), have made needlecraft in the home almost unnecessary, but I do not doubt that if the modern young housewife really had to do it she would soon become adept. Hardship and poverty bring out the best in all of us, and necessity is a through if bitter teacher. I will conclude by asking my readers to give three cheers for modern comforts....and life on social service.

Athletic Sheep

"Some blokes", remarked Uncle Harry, "Can get away with anything".

"Thinking about politicians, bureaucrats, barristers or Hitler?", I asked.

Harry fired up his pipe and spat disgustedly. "That's some of them. And they never seem to get caught. And if they do it's long after the damage is done. Remember Bill Shakespeare's remark. "The mess a bloke makes keeps on stinkin' after he snuffs it", or words to that effect. But most of 'em are big time criminals. I was thinkin' of a small time thief named Joe Lifter. I've mentioned him before to-day. Steal the bridle off a nightmare".

"Now one hot day, Joe was drivin' across Galathera plain in a lorry with a stock float on the back. He comes on to a mob of sheep, unattended. Two of 'em are tangled in an old nettin' fence, and can't get free. Joe pulls up and goes over to release 'em, then decides his effort is worth somethin', so he drops the sheep in the float. Off he goes, bold as brass, and pulls up in Belatta for a beer. When he comes out a cocky and a copper are waitin' in front of the pub, eyin' Joe's lorry".

"Those sheep are mine", says the cocky in an ominous voice. "What are you doing with them?"

"What sheep?", says Joe, lookin' perplexed. The copper points to 'em. "Holy Smoke!" says Joe. "I didn't see 'em jump in the lorry. I came through a big mob of sheep back on Galathera, and they rushed all round the lorry. Two big Alsatian dogs was chasin' 'em. Them two there must have been smarter than the rest, and jumped into the float to escape".

"Do you mean to tell me that sheep can jump over rails ten feet high," says the cop.

Joes gives a big disarmin' grin. "Haven't you seen the performin' sheep in Wirth's Circus, constable? They jump higher than ten feet".

"The cop had never been to Wirth's Circus. Neither

75

had Joe. But the limb of the law was half convinced. Joe saw he was gainin' an advantage, and he turns to the cocky. "If I was you, boss he says, "I'd get out to that mob of yours. Those Alsatians could have a lot of 'em killed by now. Grab these two and take 'em with yer".

"A look of fear shows on the farmer's face. "By cripes, you could be right", he says in a scared voice. He grabs the two sheep, ties their legs and puts 'em in the boot of his car. Then him and the cop take off full speed for Galathera. Joes goes the other way as fast as possible.

"So yer see, boy", Harry concluded," Joe was a bloke who could get away with anything, even the promotion of performin' sheep".

"Like the sheep in Wirth's Circus", I said. "Did you ever see them".

"No, I didn't, Harry grinned. "Nor did anybody else".

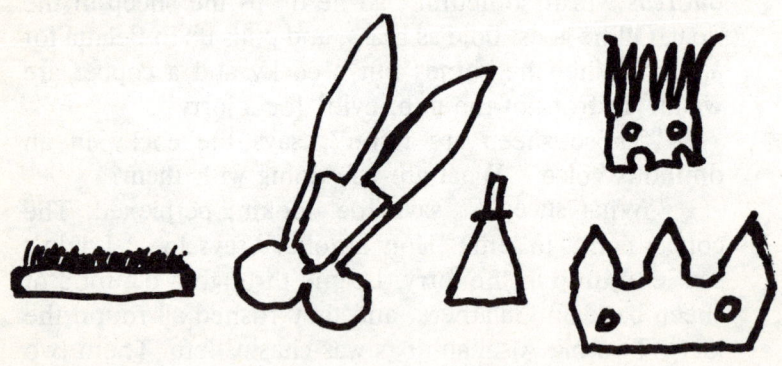

The Carnivorous Tree

"Do you think it a fact that certain trees in the Far East eat flies and bees and things"? I asked Uncle Harry. "I read an article about a plant called the drosera that grows in Borneo. When a fly or bee goes into one of its blooms, the flower closes and digests the insect, or something to that effect. Sounds a bit over the fence to me".

"Not at all, the old boy replied. "There are carnivorous trees in the mystic East that devour bigger game than insects".

"How do you know", I said scornfully. "You've never been in the mystic East to find out".

Harry began to fill his pipe. "Let me tell you of an experience of mine", he said. "A terrifyin' happenin' that took place in the Pilliga Scrub some years ago.

'Me and Stevo were roo shootin', and one day we were sneakin' through the bush lookin' for marsoopils, when we come on to this tree. It wasn't like any tree we'd ever seen before. Real dazzlin' green, with a big red flower on the end of every bough. Stevo's dog Bootlace rushes up to the tree to inspect the big heap of bones that lay all round the trunk. Like lightnin' a branch reaches out, and two great claws grabs the hound round the neck. We tried to rescue him, but a whole host of boughs reach out their claws for us, and we had to retreat. Poor old Bootlace was a goner. We watched the claws strip the flesh off him and absorb it through the stems of the flowers. Soon his bones were all that was left, and they joined the skeletons on the ground. And what a mixed heap there was.

"There was the skeleton of a horse, saddle still attached, and a pair of Baxter boots one on each side of it, so I reckon some ringer must have rode under the tree, and man and steed both went. There were a couple of moulderin' swags announced the end of two swagmen who got careless. And sheep, cow and kangaroo bones all mixed up. Stevo is lookin' at me kind of scared, and I didn't wonder".

"Looks like a man-eatin' tree, mate", he says. "We gotter kill it somehow".

"We can't get near it to cut it down, mate", I says. "It's claws would have us before we made one chop".

"We can't get wood in close enough to burn it", Stevo says. "But I got an idea that might work. Let's go back to camp".

"On the way back Stevo shoots a small roo. He was hardly big enough to skin, but I was to find out he was part of Stevo's plan to kill the monster. He prepares the carcase, and we takes it back to the tree. Usin' long poles we pushed it under the deadly boughs without gettin' too close ourselves. Believe me, it didn't take long for the meat on that little roo to get devoured. We went back to camp hopin' the plan would work as Stevo reckoned.

"Next mornin' we goes to investigate, and finds our hopes are fulfilled. The tree's dead and withered, the blooms fallin' off it and limbs hangin' down on the ground".

"What brought this about?" I queried.

Harry gave a cunning smile. "Stevo had a tin of poison called Destroyzit, that he painted on the roo skins to keep the weevils out. It was guaranteed to kill all insects and all types of vegetation. He filled the roo's carcase with it. Exit the man eatin' tree".

"How did the tree get there in the first place?" I queried.

"Easy answered," the old boy replied. "One of our migratory birds was returnin' from the mystic East, and he carried a seed. He dropped it when he was passin' over the Pilliga Scrub, and from that seed the tree grew".

"How come more trees didn't grow from seeds off the original," I asked.

"Tropical trees have a male and female", Harry said. 'Unless there's a pair the seeds are not fertile".

Harry had an answer for everything. I gave up, wondering where he read about carnivorous trees and fungus.

The Saga of Sam Fat

"The Irish are a pretty superstitious race", I remarked to Uncle Harry. "Believe in goblins and banshees and things".

"It's a fact", Harry agreed. "Just the same, some of 'em have a realistic outlook, and laugh at superstition, religious or otherwise. And the same can be said of the Chinese.

"I remember one time years ago I was workin' at a little minin' town called Tinville. A lot of Chinese were there fossickin' for the tin. One very cunnin' old cove had a store and restaurant. His name was Sam Fat, and he was a great con man. Just out of town two other Chinese had a bit of a poultry farm. Their names were Sum Pong and Sum Poo.

"Anyway Sum Pong ups and dies. Sum Poo decides to give him a big slap-up funeral, with gifts left on the grave at night, in the old Chinese belief that the gods expected a hand-out to help the departed into Heaven. So Sum Poo goes to see Sum Fat about dressin' and cookin' some fouls as a gift for the gods.

"No need bling fows", Sam Fat in pidgin. "Me gottee plenty fows in ice-box. Come tomollow he be cooked leady".

"That night Sam sneaks out to Sum Poo's fowl-yard and burns a bit of sulphur on a shovel. Half a dozen chooks tumble down stunned, and Sam whisks 'em off to his restaurant, where he prepares 'em. Next day he sells 'em to Sum Poo, who puts 'em on his brother's grave at nightfall.

"Next day the fowls are gone, and Sum Poo is real happy, thinkin' that the gods have accepted his offering. He goes back to Sam Fat for more chooks. Same result that night.

"After three nights, Sum Poo reckons eighteen chooks are enough to placate any form of god, so he gave up the nightly presentation. He didn't know there was only ever six fowls, and no god ever got 'em.''

"What was the story to it", I asked.

Harry grinned around his pipe. ''Sam Fat used to go down after dark and bring the chooks home. Not satisfied with stealin' 'em off Sum Poo, he sold the same six chooks three times. Yer see, Sam Fat feared no god and follered no religion only money. As I told yer earlier, a realistic outlook is more profitable than a religious one''.

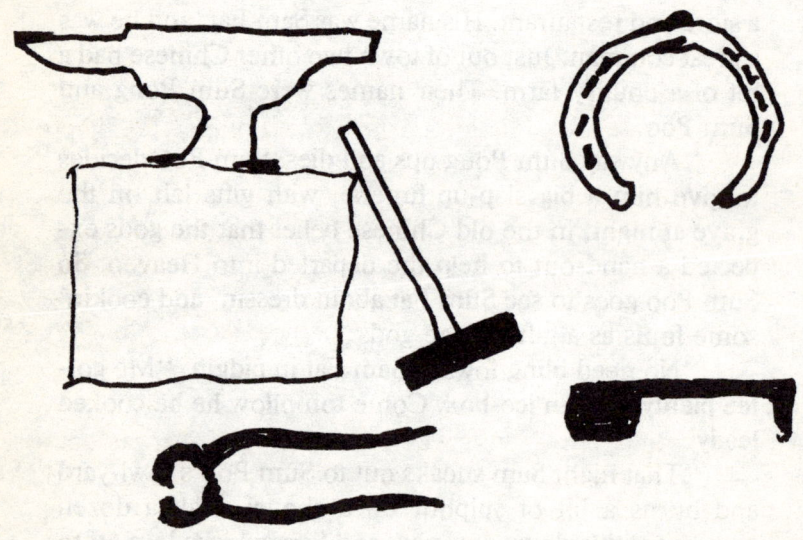

The Ghost of the Aloes

"It ain't a good thing to take ghost yarns seriously", said Uncle Harry. "Ignorant people tell yer about spirits of the dead comin' back to earth possessed of sooper-natcheral powers. A lot of bull, worse than the tall tales in the newspapers. It's the livin' yer gotter fear, not the dead. Ghost stories can only cause yer trouble if yer take notice of 'em".

"Are you speaking from experience?", I asked.

"My oath I am", Harry replied. "I'll tell yer about it, boy. Me and Stevo were once foolish enough to swaller a ghost yarn.

"We was off to pick up a mob of cattle west of Moree. We decides to camp at Gum Flat reserve, near a big dense clump of aloe bushes. We'd often heard there was a ghost in 'em, the spirit of a woman who'd been murdered there years before. Old timers swore that horses would never go near 'em, because they were scared of the phantom that came there at night. So we hobbled our horses and camped a good half mile from the haunted aloes.

"Comes mornin', and when we wake up there's no horses to be seen. They were always good campers, and we couldn't work out where they've gone. It was open country, nothin' in sight only the big clump of aloes, dark and sinister lookin' ".

"They've cleared out", Stevo says. "They must have gone close to the aloes, mate. You can bet the ghost put 'em off camp".

"Yer reasonin's pretty sound", I agrees.

"We grabs a bridle each, and Stevo goes east and I heads west.

"Now I tell yer, boy, I walked 'til dinner-time and didn't see hide or hair of a horse. I suffers the long trudge back to camp, and puts the billy on. Soon I see Stevo comin'. He'd had no luck either.

"They've really vanished", I says. "The ghost must have scared 'em for miles".

"Stevo doesn't reply, and I looks up to see him standin' with his mouth open, sort of petrified. He's pointin' a shakin' finger at the aloes. What d'yer reckon he could see, boy?"

"The ghost, I suppose", I replied.

"Not on yer life", Harry said in a disgusted tone. "Our horses. They'd been standin' in the aloes all night and most of the mornin'. Now they were hungry, and had decided to walk out of their cover and start grazin'.

"So now yer can see that ghosts are pretty over-rated animals. So beware of all bloody sooperstitions, and the thick-headed yokels who believe in 'em".

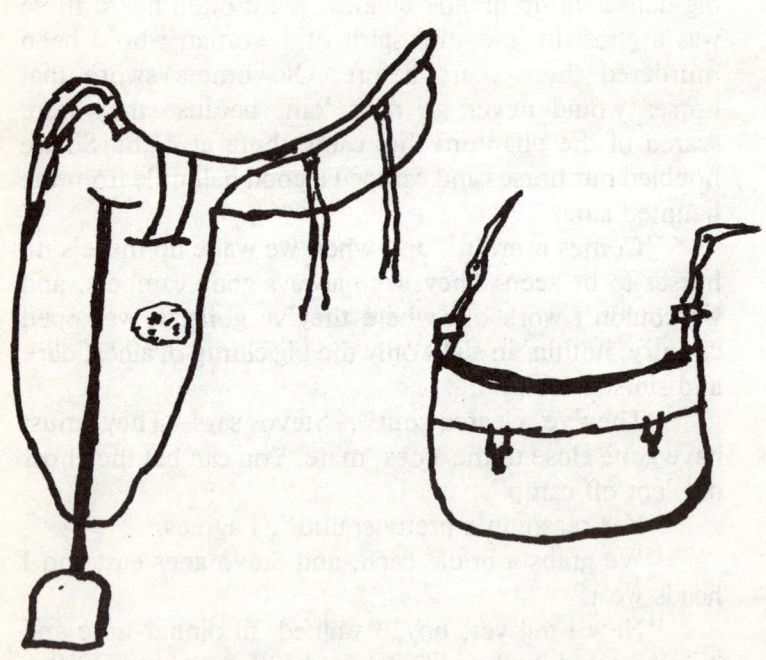

The Milk-Fed Koala

"Koalas", said Uncle Harry, "are quaint little mar-soopils. But they can be sneaky and deceitful. Yer wouldn't reckon they'd steal, would yer?"

"Hardly", I replied.

"I'll tell yer a story about a real dibolicul little bear", Harry began.

"Me and Stevo were camped out in Mungel Scrub, doin' a bit of ringbarkin'. We had a nanny-goat we used to milk every mornin'. Nothin' like a bit of goat's milk to give yer stamina.

"Up in the fork of a nearby gum a little koala used to sit. He wasn't annoyin' us, or so we thought, so we left him alone.

"One mornin' I goes to milk the goat, and finds she's bone dry. I reports to Stevo, and he's real misty-fied too. There was plenty of green feed around, so it seemed a bit strange.

"Next mornin' there's no milk again, but all around where I had the goat tethered there's little paw marks. Me gaze went to the limb where the bear was asleep, his little tummy bulgin'. Over to the tree I goes, and in the hollow at the bottom I finds a fruit tin, one we had threw away after eatin' the contents. There's dregs of goat milk in the bottom. I got awful suspicious and commandeered the tin.

"The moon rose about ten o'clock that night. Me and Stevo are watchin', and sure enough down comes the bear, and starts searchin' for the fruit tin, but he can't find it. Stevo had a chaff-bag ready. A quick rush, a short struggle, and the bear is in the bag.

Harry paused to light his pipe, then continued.

"We took that bear nearly ten miles away and let him go, and unlike General Macarthur he didn't return. We go out full quota of goat's milk after that".

"You don't mean to say the koala was milking the

goat?" I asked. "No other answer", Harry replied. "That little bear was livin' on the milk of human kindness. There's some very imaginative creatures in the bush, I can tell yer".

"There's some very imaginative humans, too", I replied, but Harry only grinned around his pipe and remained silent.

Reptile Repercussions

"Yer read silly rot in magazines about how goannas are good to eat", announced Uncle Harry. "And now there's films that show blokes eatin' 'em. What a heap of tripe. The stinkin' cows live on carrion, and when yer cut one open he's full of stinkin' yeller fat that' turn the guts of a starvin' dog. Whoever started the "Goanna for grub" fable is an unmitigated liar, and yer known how I dislike covers who tell tall tales.

"Me and Stevo was doin' a stick pickin' job once, and our mate was a big tough bloke we called Blocky, because he was solid in build and solid in the head too. He was a feller could eat anything. Raw bacon, mouldy bread, tainted meat, he took 'em all in his stride. Must have had a copper paunch and stainless steel intestines. Never had a belly ache in his life. Stevo reckoned he was like an emu, could digest bolts and nuts if he had to.

"We were goin' well at the job when heavy rain fell and the river rose. We couldn't get to town and we'd been out of meat for two days. This went hard with Blocky, who was real carnivorous. Stevo and me took our rifles and went lookin' for a roo or a wallaby. Blocky stayed at the camp, with his tongue out for the taste of meat. "I'm gettin' weak", he says. "If yer don't get a roo I won't see tomorrer mornin' ".

"Stevo and me were gone all afternoon, and when we get back with a wallaby a piece there's no movement at the camp. "Watch out mate", Steveo says. "When he smells these marsoopils he'll eat 'em raw".

"When we goes in the tent we gets a hell of a shock. Here's Blocky layin' on his swag, three shades whiter than a starched shirt, lookin' as if he's been dead for a week. Beside him is the fryin-pan, with a horrible lookin' yeller concoction in it. Stevo took a sniff and nearly fainted. "Goanna mate", he gasps.

"Blocky speaks in a weak whisper. "I couldn't wait

85

for yer to shoot somethin', so I skittled a googar and made a stew. Oney had a couple of mouthfuls and it downed me''.

"Stevo always used drastic measures to cure the sick, halt and lame. He half fills a pannikin out of brine-cask, tops it off with hot sauce and pours the lot inter Blocky. We carried him outside and he starts to vomit. After he burps up all the goanna gravy and cetra he looks a bit better. But it was a week before he got completely right, and he had a bad relapse when a goanna was seen passin' the camp. But he survived.

"If he survived Stevo's antidote he could no doubt survive anything", I remarked.

"Stevo' cure, though severe was the deciding factor between life and death for Blocky", Harry said wisely. "Why d'yer think Mother Nature scrapped the age of reptiles? I'll tell yer. Because all the cave-men were dyin' off from eatin' the ancestors of the present-day goannas. Remember the snake in the garden of Eden? Reptiles of any sort can cause continuous strife and repercussions. If Adam was alive he'd verify me statement".

The Pig and the Grindstone

"Never ever believe", said Uncle Harry, "that pigs are not intelligent animals".

"They always strike me as being lazy and moronic", I said. "Eat all tucker in the world as long as you cart it to their sty. Then they go to sleep".

"That's true of domestic pigs", Harry agreed, "but the wild pig, the feller who has to strive to survive, is a different type altogther. He's cunning, aggressive and without fear. And a fighter when challenged.

"I remember one time me and Steveo were rabbitin' in a pretty wild place. We were camped at the shearer's huts, and just over behind the dunny was a big grindstone on a stand, a relic of the blade days when the old guns used it to sharpen the shears. It had fallen into decay since machines had been installed in the shed.

"The squatter came to our camp the first day, and gave us a grim warnin'. "There's a savage boar pig lives hereabouts", he says. "Got an awful set on rabbiters. He chased the last lot off the place. Look out for him".

"We made the camp secure, and went to bed early in preparation for settin' traps the next day. Some time in the night I woke up. It was bright moonlight, and I can hear a queer sound comin' from the direction of the dunny. A harsh scrapin' noise like a knife bein' sharpened on a steel. I got quietly out of bed and snuck over towards the dunny. The sound became clearer, then stopped suddenly. I'm nearly to the dunny when out from behind it comes a huge boar pig with his tusks shinin' in the light of the moon. In a split second he's chargin' at me!

I took off for the huts at a record breakin' pace, but the pig was gainin' at every yard, and I reckoned me number was goin' up. I could feel the hog's hot breath on the seat of me underpants!

"Just then there was a stripe of fire and a loud report from the huts, and I knew Stevo was in action with his reliable old Winchester. The bullet missed me ribs by a sixteenth of an inch, and plows inter the pig's brain.

"Stevo steps out the door holdin' the smokin' rifle. "Risky shot mate", he says, "but I pulled her off. Better a bullet in the pig's head than a tusk in yer testicles".

"We examined the carcase next mornin', and he had the longest sharpest tusks you ever saw. "Wonder how he got 'em that sharp", I says.

Stevo suggests that we foller his tracks, and we did just that. They led us straight to the grindstone, and what made the pig's tusks sharp was easy to see. All along the side of the grindstone were the scratches where he'd been sharpenin' his stabbers. I knew then what the scrapin' noise was that woke me up. That old boar was really pre-parin' for hostilities with us. But his weapons wuz limited to hand to hand warfare. Stevo and the Winchester was somethin' he couldn't cope with".

A Cure for Sore Feet

"Yer hear of a lot of cures for sore feet", said Uncle Harry. "The best thing of all is common pig-lard without any salt in it. Used regular, it'll soften the hooves of a donkey.

"I remember an old swaggie we called Bendy, who used to hump his drum long distances. He always had his boots filled with lard. Shoot an old wild boar and get the fat out of him. Now yer aware how rank an old boar smells. When Bendy got warmed up yer couldn't get near him for the stink. Get down wind of him on a hot day when he took his boots off, and you'd nearly ger asphyxiated. But he never had sore feet.

"Then there was a bloke used to rub his feet with goanna oil, which is a dangerous and sinister unguent. He gave up this practice when his toes started to resemble claws, and black and yeller stripes appeared on his feet. A few applications of lard put him right again.

"Toby was an old whaler who always rubbed his feet with metho. One day after givin' his right foot a good dose, he lights his pipe and drops the match. Result, a badly scorched foot that put him on crutches for a week. He used lard and was O.K.

Harry was warming to his task. "This simple cure", he continued, "is also beneficial to the feet of bush creatures. One day Stevo and me were punchin' the teams along a hard, rocky track, and we sees a big centipede comin'. He must have travelled a long way, because his tongue was hangin' out and he was limpin' somethin' terrible. Stevo smeared the inside of a treacle tin with lard, and coaxed him into it. All night long that centipede walked round and round inside that tin, his sore feet absorbin' the wonderful curative power of the lard. Next day he didn't show a sign of lameness in any of his hundred feet. He was fairly trottin' as he left the camp.

"A great thing in the favour of lard is that it ain't expensive. Not like the fancy ointments and salves yer buy at the chemists' shops. Yer can get lard for next door to nuthin'. Leaves yer cash to buy beer with, and that beer can be soothin' yer system while the lard soothes yer sore feet. There's nothin' like bein' practical, boy''.